Eye for an Eye

A Colby Tate Mystery
Book 2

Allen Kent

For information address AllenPearce Publishers,
16635 Hickory Drive, Neosho, MO 64850

AllenPearce Publishers ©  ©

Library of Congress Cataloging-in-Publication Data
Allen Kent
The Talisman Murder
Kent, Allen

ISBN:
ISBN-13: 978-1-7332173-7-8

DEDICATION

To my Southwest Missouri friends whose
stories of Ozark characters added such fun and
interest to this book

ACKNOWLEDGMENTS

Grateful thanks to my team of readers: my wife Holly, Diane Andris, Juliet Scherer, and Judy Day. You all made this a much better book. And special thanks to Uvi Poznansky for her cover design.

1

The two ancient women hunched together, gazing intently with filmy silver eyes into the cup between them.

"Ohhh, Edith," one whispered in a high chirp, gripping her sister's hand beneath the table. "Do you see it there in the leaves? By the handle?"

Her sister's face tightened into a wrinkled frown. "I see it, Ethel. I was hoping I wasn't reading it just right." Both looked up from the flowered porcelain bowl at the stout, dark-eyed woman who sat across the cloth-draped table beside a teenaged girl whose features were a prettier version of her mother's. The woman fidgeted nervously. The girl had been relaxing back on her spindle-backed wooden chair with a look of tolerant boredom, but leaned quickly forward.

It had taken twenty minutes to drive to the base of the wooded hill and the path that led to the old women's cabin, then another ten to climb the quarter mile to their door. The session was approaching its second hour and the girl had been absently running through her mind the list of things she would rather be doing. It was a Saturday. Three of her friends had invited her to a float trip on Mill Creek. A girlfriend wanted to run up to Springfield to shop. Even her unfinished physiology homework seemed a more interesting alternative. But her mother spoke little English and the girl had been trained from childhood to be patient and obedient.

The ceremony had begun with the aged twin sisters preparing tea for four: a dark, loose-leafed Turkish blend that the mother provided after being counseled by a friend that the old women of the woods preferred a tea that reflected the tastes of the supplicant. The sisters steeped and poured it unstrained into the flowered cups, rounder and deeper than the delicate glass tea service the Arab girl was accustomed to. She and her mother had added cubes of sugar. The four women sipped leisurely at the strong, dark drink while the girl explained on behalf of her mother why she wished to have a reading.

"Our family has been away from our home in Ariha—that's in Syria—for over a year now. We have heard nothing from our family: my grandparents or my mother's brothers. Mother was told by a woman at the church we go to in Crayton that sometimes you can see what is happening in people's lives."

The old women had smiled and nodded in unison, encouraging the mother to sip until less than a teaspoon of liquid remained. They showed her how to carefully tip the few drops of tea out onto a saucer, then positioned the empty cup between them. As mirror images of each other, they gazed down at the dregs.

There had been a long pause before the woman who called herself Ethel spoke her concern. Her silver-white hair had thinned to wispy strands that gave her spotted head the appearance of being surrounded by a drifting halo. A bristly tuft of coarse gray whiskers sprang from the right side of her chin, just as an identical tuft marked the left side of her sister's wrinkled jaw. The girl sat forward at the alarm in the woman's voice, her mother leaning with her.

"What do they see?" the older woman asked in Arabic.

Edith answered without needing translation. "We begin our readings at the handle," she said in a strained whisper. "It is often the message of greatest importance."

". . . and?" the girl prompted, her mother looking over at her nervously.

"And there has been a death," Ethel said solemnly.

The mother gasped and covered her lips with a trembling hand. "Is it family? Can you see who it is?"

The sisters looked at each other for confirmation, shaking their heads in unison. "We cannot see who it is," Edith said. "But it is someone from your home. Someone close. You will know soon."

2

The explosion jolted me upright and into a cold sweat. I had been lost in a dream of the PTSD damned, crouching tensely forward as my squad led a sweep through some unidentified desert town. I had interrogated the village elders and learned nothing when a boy beckoned from an alley. "Follow me," he said in a loud whisper. "There is a house in the next street where Al Qaeda is making bombs. I will show you the house."

"Why didn't the village elders tell me?" I called after the boy as he ran ahead through a narrow cross alley with mud walls pressing down on us from both sides.

"The elders are being watched. One of the men with them is always a spy. They are afraid to tell you anything."

He pointed toward a two-story house of ochre brick, separated from the street by a head-high compound wall, its top laced with broken glass. "There," he whispered. "You will find them in there. But be quick. If they know you are coming, they will blow up the house."

The squad split and I followed my squadron leader to the grilled, wrought iron gate that opened into the courtyard. He reached across for the latch and lifted it silently. The explosion that followed jarred me back into a sweat-soaked bed and fully awake.

I twisted to the edge and glanced at the red digits of my bedside clock. 4:15 a.m. Instinctively, I replayed and analyzed the sound. Too full and deep for kids setting off fireworks down at the fishing access to the creek below the house. And it had been followed by the telltale rumble of destruction. Something had exploded with enough force to shake the house like a minor quake.

I switched on the lamp and was wrestling on my jeans when my cell erupted with the opening bars of the theme song from "The Great Escape." Not a call from someone in the department. That would have been "The Magnificent Seven." In Crayton, people have pretty well learned to bypass 911 and call straight to my phone. The local cell prefix, plus aces and eights. 1188. In a poor attempt at humor by our locally owned phone company, the numbers had been assigned to both me and the sheriff's office, just with different prefixes.

I cleared my throat and tried to answer as if I'd been waiting up for the call. "Sheriff Tate."

"Tate, this is Lonnie Heiskell." He was shouting into his phone. "I'm working as night watchman over here at the creek water project. Somebody just blew the thing up."

"Easy, Lonnie," I said. "You're yelling so loud I can hardly understand you. Someone blew what up?"

"*The dam*," he bellowed into my ear. "Someone blew up the damn dam."

Lonnie's family moved to Crayton when we were both in the ninth grade. My clearest boyhood memory of him was of his offer to barter a week's lunch money if I'd let him copy my algebra test answers. I'd agreed, slipped him my paper five minutes before the end of the period, and pocketed two-fifty. Mrs. Swisher called us both into her classroom after school the next day, sat us on opposite sides of her desk, and gave us new tests—different questions. I'd done okay. Lonnie missed them all. We both went home with a note that led to my butt getting chewed by my mother and Uncle Jack taking a belt to me. That was the last time I thought it smart to sell information. Lonnie didn't look any the worse for wear when I saw him the next morning. He was basically a good kid. Just bone lazy. Never could hold a job for long. Right now, he sounded wound pretty tight.

"Are you okay, Lonnie? Anybody injured?"

"No. The guard shack's up on the hill above the creek. But I had some rocks fall on the roof, and one come damn close to near killin' me. Another busted out the window of my pickup. I'm okay. But it scared the shit out of me."

"Sit tight, Lonnie. I'll be there in ten minutes. Have you called the company people?"

"No. I called you first thing. It just happened."

"Yeah. I heard it," I told him and grabbed for my uniform shirt. My Sig and holster hung on a wooden peg beside the bedroom door and were buckled on before I reached the mudroom and my boots.

As I drove the three miles to the dam site, I radioed Bobby Lule. Bobby's our deputy who roams the county between midnight and when we open the office at 8 a.m. He's also an ex-Marine, a solitary guy whose personal manifestation of PTSD inclines him to want to be alone. But when trouble raises its ugly head in the dark hours of early morning, Bobby's not shy about facing it down and calling for help when he needs it. When I reached him, he said he'd been at Casey's having a cup of coffee with Darren Sykes, the night patrol officer for the Crayton police, but had heard the explosion and was headed east.

"I thought I'd hear from you," he said through the radio. "I couldn't pinpoint the sound and didn't see no light in the sky. Thought maybe a meth lab had blown up. But I figured you'd get a call and could tell me where I needed to be."

"The new dam site," I told him. "Lonnie Heiskell called and said someone blew up the dirt work that's been done."

"What the hell was Lonnie doing out there?"

"They've hired him as night watchman."

"Hmm," Bobby grunted. "Good job for him, 'long as nothing happens. I'm about five minutes away."

"About the same for me. I'll meet you at the gate."

Bobby's headlights were right behind me when I pulled up to the guard shack that protected a sixteen-foot rolling gate in a chain link fence that disappeared off into the dark in both directions. Chunks of rock littered the scraped lot outside the fence as if it had rained boulders.

I'd swung by the site within a day of Mid-Missouri Water first putting up the fence. There wasn't much to see from the gate and no real reason to get official and try to talk my way down into the hollow to see how construction was coming along. The plan was to back up Mill Creek, the stream that runs below my place, creating a 1500-acre lake to replace a city water supply that depended on two wells that either needed to go deeper or be replaced. The whole process has created one of the messiest public rows since I came back to Crayton three years ago.

As far upstream as I am, it won't do much more than widen the creek and improve fishing. But for the folks who own bottomland in Blackjack Holler, it means losing property that's been in families for generations through eminent domain. Tempers have been running at a low boil for nearly a year now. Even town folk who aren't losing property aren't thrilled that some of their neighbors are having theirs taken away and can't do anything about it. Lots of this land, including the patch up along Huckleberry Ridge where I grew up, isn't much more than limestone bedrock covered by enough clay to support hardwood forest and a little pasture grass. Good for raising cattle, but not much more than that. But it was homesteaded by hardy, independent folk five generations back. Those who've come after them are just as stubborn and don't take kindly to being told someone can just up and buy their land without their say. And the river bottom along Blackjack Holler is some of the best in the county.

Lonnie was standing beside my Explorer before I could push the door open.

"Thanks for getting here so fast, Tate," he stammered, stumbling backward as I forced him out of the way and climbed from the patrol car. Bobby Lule joined us. I led them both toward the sliding gate that had been pushed halfway open.

"So, Lonnie. Tell us what happened."

He pressed so close as we walked that I found myself veering away. He reminded me of an old birddog I'd once had who was so frightened by gunshots I kept tripping over him when my friends were out squirrel hunting within earshot of our place.

"I was just sitting in the shed there, watching a video I'd loaded onto my laptop—the company don't mind me doing that—when there was this huge explosion. The shed's just sitting on skids, and I thought it was going to tip over. Rocked it up off the skids and half turned it. Then dirt and rocks started raining down. One came right through the roof. About a hundred-pounder, I'd say. Missed me by maybe a foot and smashed the hell out of my computer. Damn near killed me." He pointed at a ragged hole in the shingled roof of the guardhouse. "And another took out my windshield." A white Dodge Ram sat beside the shed with a few mosaic patches of glass clinging to the edges of the window frame.

"You been down there?" Bobby asked, forcing the gate open another six feet.

"Yeah. But I called you first, Tate. Then called Mr. Spangler who owns the construction company. He's up in Springfield so won't get down here for at least another hour. Then I walked on down to see what I could see. I only had my flashlight, and it's pitch dark down there. But what they'd got done on the dam is pretty much blowed apart."

I inched away from the clinging security man. "How much did they have done, Lonnie?"

"Not a lot, really. They'd diverted the creek through a concrete culvert that they can close up when the dam's done and had started moving dirt. Maybe four or five feet on top of the culvert. But I don't think it's even a third done."

The guard shack and fence were on the ridge above the construction site, with a gravel road that descended into the narrow valley on the downstream side of the dam. Another patch of ground had been cleared inside the fence and held an assortment of graders, dozers, and dump trucks. A dirt film covered the equipment, with one truck and dozer marred by deep craters in their yellow hoods. We swept the road with three lights as we moved down toward the creek, the rubble thickening as we got closer to the dam.

The explosion had thrown up a chest-high berm along the creek bed and we clambered up onto it, gazing down into what was now a half-acre pond. There was no sign of the concrete bypass.

"*Damn*," Bobby muttered, flashing his light around the edges of the crater. "Haven't seen nothing like this since I-raq. This was quite an explosion."

I ran my own beam along the far bank, then into the broken trees around us. "And pretty well centered on the dam," I added. "I was thinking on the way over here that some storage shed must have been storing dynamite and blown up. But this was set off right in the middle of the dam. No accident."

"Nobody came by me, and the gate was closed all night," Lonnie insisted defensively, pressing back against my elbow.

"You unlocked the gate when you came down?"

"Yeah. It was chained and padlocked. I had the key in the shed and had to unlock it."

"We'll check the fence when it gets light to see if it's been cut," I told him. "But as I remember, this fence doesn't surround the site. Just stretches along the road for about a quarter mile in each direction."

Lonnie nodded in the dark. "Yeah. It's mainly to keep people from trying to steal stuff like gas or mess with the equipment. You could come in around it pretty easy—or come down through the trees on the other side of the creek."

"You didn't hear anything down here?"

"No." He frowned down into the crater. "But I probably wouldn't. You don't hear much in the shack. And I was watching one of them *Fast and Furious* movies. Like I told you, they don't mind me watching that stuff while I'm on the job. I'm just there to keep people from trying to break in through the gate at night."

I turned upstream along the edge of the berm. "Let's have a quick look around for anything obvious," I said to Bobby. "Then wait for daylight and Mr. Spangler to get here. We don't want to tramp around too much in the dark, and he'll be able to give us a lot better idea of what we're seeing when it gets light." Bobby grunted his agreement and headed along the berm in the other direction. Lonnie Heiskell remained planted where we left him, not sure whose side to cling to. I'd looped around to where the stream poured into the newly created pool and started back toward Lonnie when Bobby called from the downstream side.

"*Tate. Better get over here.*"

"You found something?"

"Yes, Sir. We've got ourselves a body."

3

My thought as I scrambled along the edge of the crater toward Bobby's light was that whoever had blown up the dam had damn well blown himself up with it. Bobby had moved downstream and into the brush along the creek bed, much of it shredded and flattened by rock shrapnel from the blast. Bobby's shout had jarred Lonnie into motion and he joined me below the crater, pressed uncomfortably close to one elbow. As I neared, I could tell this wasn't a body that had met its untimely end during the night.

"I smelled something as I got down this way," Bobby called as I approached. "Followed my nose and found this. Almost didn't see it up there." He flashed his light up into a white oak that had been sturdy enough to withstand the explosion.

The body was draped over a thick branch, face-down, about ten feet above the ground. As it had tumbled through the upper limbs, some of the man's clothing had been ripped away, leaving the stomach and chest up to the shoulders exposed. With three flashlights shining up at the corpse, it was clear the man had been dead a few days. The clothing that remained was caked in dirt, and there were early signs of decomposition.

Lonnie turned quickly away, choking back what was left of a night of snacking on Coke and Cheetos in the guard shack. I dropped my beam to eye level. Bobby and I had seen a lot of death. But Lonnie had taken a job as a night watchman feeling pretty confident it wouldn't expose him to any more mayhem than he got from his smash and crash chase movies.

"Let's get back to the cars and get some masks and a kit. Bobby, you call Grace and Frankie and get them up. Tell them I need them over here as fast as they can make it. And ask them both to bring their pickups and a ladder if they have one. Then give Chase a call and tell him we need a coroner and his ambulance. Lonnie, you'd better call your boss. Let him know there's a body. He might want to bring down some of his company people."

We made our way back up through the gate to the patrol cars. Bobby called the other deputies while I pulled gloves, masks, and an evidence kit from the back of the Explorer. Then we waited for better light and a way to get our mystery man down from his roost.

Frankie lives up in the north part of the county, a good thirty minutes away. Grace has an apartment behind her parents' place on the edge of town, though sometimes you'll find her staying with her unfortunate choice of a boyfriend, Sal Beccera. She must have been at home because she beat Frankie to the dam site by fifteen minutes, driving her dad's Tundra with ten and twelve-foot ladders jutting from the back of the bed.

"I was dressed," she said as she climbed from the pickup. "I heard the boom and your call to Bobby. Figured you might want me coming in early."

Grace is my chief deputy, a Latina known to most people around Crayton as Amazing Grace: partly because of her fearless police work, and partly because she's the kind of woman you'd expect to see sitting beside a fire along the beach in some commercial for Corona Lite. Tall. Raven-haired. Dark eyes that give meaning to the word "smoldering" when she gets nettled about something. And a face that turns heads even among those who see her every day in town. And yes. There's always a ripple of talk around Crayton about a single sheriff and a chief deputy who looks like Grace, even though she has a boyfriend who guards her like a sheepdog, believes she has no place being a cop, and shouldn't be trying to "rise above her raising'."

Grace glanced about at the rock garden of a parking area and the broken roof of the guard shack, then back at the ladders in her truck. "We going to be climbing down into something?" she asked.

"Up," I corrected. "Grab your evidence kit and one of the ladders and follow me." I turned to Lonnie. "You better stay up here. Send Ritter and Chase Backman down as soon as they get here." He didn't object.

The late-June sun was just beginning to paint a glow across the eastern horizon as I led Grace and Bobby back down the road and into the trees along the lower creek. As we neared the body, Grace's nose wrinkled, and she stopped to pull a cloth mask from her kit.

"Bobby didn't say anything about a body," she called after me. I stopped to wait for her to catch up.

"He didn't want all the people around town with scanners to come racing over here. Asking you to bring a ladder won't cause nearly the excitement we'd get if we said somebody'd been killed." I pointed through the growing light at the body suspended from the oak.

"*Madre de Dios*," Grace muttered, gazing up at the corpse. "What happened here?"

"Someone blew up the dam."

She dropped the ladder she was carrying, turned to look at the banks of broken earth where the beginnings of the dam had been, then back at the body. "Do you think this was a result of the explosion?"

I stood the taller of the ladders up behind the dead man. "We'll know when we get the body down. But from here, I'd say it's pretty clear the person's been dead a few days. My fear is that the body was buried in the dam and was thrown over here when it blew up."

Grace moved her ladder to a position below the man's head. We stood for a moment, looking grimly at each other.

I slipped on a mask and gloves. "Do you want to wait until Chase gets here? He can help me bring him down."

Grace shook her head and pulled on her own mask, answering through the thick layers of material. "Chase is too old to be climbing up there to help you hoist that body over the limb. I'll do it. We can lower him down to Bobby."

Lule had been systematically working his way around the draped corpse, photographing it from below. He handed me the camera as I started up the ladder. "Get some from up close, then have Grace do the same," he suggested. "Once we begin to move it, a lot of things might change."

Up in the parking area, two other vehicles pulled into the lot. The coroner, I guessed, and our other day-deputy, Frankie Ritter.

I climbed to where I could photograph the swollen legs and back, then handed the camera to Grace who grimaced behind the mask. "Everything's covered with dirt," she muttered. "I think you're right about the body being buried. And . . . Oh, my God, Tate. This man's been shot. Right in the middle of the forehead. Most of the back of his head's gone." She snapped a few more photos and lowered the camera to Bobby.

Chase Backman followed Frankie through the trees to the ladders, both mumbling something I couldn't pick up as they stared up at the body. Chase is what folks around Crayton call our "provider of full-service dying." In addition to being coroner, he owns and operates the ambulance service, runs the assisted living center, and is the town's only funeral director. But nobody would want anyone else taking care of them during their final days and hours. Chase is one of those guys who, if he found your wallet on the sidewalk, would return it with an extra $20 tucked inside. He's as caring and compassionate as Mother Teresa, and well enough acquainted with death that not much fazes the man. But I could tell from his mutterings that this was the first body he'd seen draped over an oak limb.

"We've got photos from every angle, Chase," I called down to him. "Looks like the guy's been shot. Anything else you want us to do before we move him?" It was becoming light enough that the men below could clearly see the corpse.

"Did you get a photo of that exposed chest area from the side?"

he asked. "See how all the darker color is up along the back? The man was lying on his back for quite a while just after he died. Long enough to go through the rigor stages face-up. Any idea how he got up there?"

"Did you hear the boom?" I called down. Chase is as deaf as a post without his hearing aids.

"No. But I felt it. Woke me up. I was waiting for a call."

"Well, someone blew up the dam. I think the body was buried in it and got thrown out by the blast. Landed in this tree."

"Well, isn't that just the damnedest thing," he muttered. "Bring him on down. Let's see what we can figure out."

Grace winced and lifted the shoulders, pushing up as I grabbed the man's belt and drew him toward me. "Better keep that head leaning forward," she choked through the mask. "It looks like a real mess."

I lowered the weight until Bobby and Frankie could grab legs and hips and ease the body carefully to the ground. Lonnie had warned the coroner to bring a body bag down to the creek, and Chase scraped an area clear of rocks and broken limbs. The three men stretched the corpse onto its back on the black plastic.

The man had a shock of thick, dark hair and a coarse mustache that turned around the corners of his purple lips. His pale skin had once been swarthy. Maybe Latino. Though the clothing had been torn and bunched as he tumbled through the tree's upper branches, they were largely intact, including one shoe. His trousers were a heavy military olive drab, the shirt long-sleeved and a plain, lighter green. The single brown shoe clung to an ankle that bulged under a brown stocking.

I handed out assignments. "Grace, go through the man's pockets and see if you can find anything that might identify him. Bobby, wait for the men from the construction company up by the gate, then look over the blast site. Find out everything you can about where they were with construction, who's been working at the site, how someone might have ended up buried in the dirt work, and who they think would have wanted to blow the thing up. And Frankie, start a back-and-forth on both sides of the creek. Look for anything that doesn't belong, even if you think it's creek trash. Stick a flag at each location and keep a numbered description of the items. See if you can find that other shoe."

I turned to Chase who was kneeling beside the corpse. "Before you bag him, tell me what you see."

He leaned back onto his haunches. "Well, for one thing, I agree that he was buried. And he's definitely been shot. Something larger than a .22. Not a shotgun. As centered as the wound is on his forehead, I'd say this is an execution-style killing. Or he was hit by someone who was one hell of a marksman." He leaned a little to the side. "I mentioned the livor mortis coloration. That tells me he was stretched out on his back for long enough that the blood pooled there and coagulated before the body was thrown into the tree. Can't tell much else until we get him cleaned up. Even then, I'll need help from the state crime lab."

Grace had been through the pockets of the man's tattered pants and was searching the broken brush and limbs around the base of the oak. "Got something here," she called, holding up a round disk about the size of a thick poker chip, attached to a short leather lace. The surface was glazed ceramic with an indigo blue outer circle around concentric white and blue rings. At its center, a pea-sized dot of the same deep blue seemed to stare back at us.

"What have you got there?" Chase stood and took it from her as she brought it over, holding it up to catch the first glint of morning sun. "Did it fall from the body?"

Grace shook her head. "I don't know. I've never seen anything like it. This mean anything to you, Tate?"

My mind had flown half a world away. I was again standing in the doorway of a mudbrick home in Iraq's Anbar province, questioning a village elder. He insisted he knew nothing about Al Qaeda activity in his village, trembling as he spoke. He was shaking, not because he was lying, but because the squad of

Marines that stood behind this American interpreter always brought trouble. Beside him, tacked to the doorframe with a rusted nail, was a woven, postcard-sized tapestry with tasseled edges. At its bottom hung an identical amulet.

"*Ya Rab*," I murmured "Yes. It means something to me." The subconscious mumbling of the Arabic phrase I'd heard so often from Adeena's lips when she was disturbed by something brought my thoughts back to the body at my feet. "It's what's called a *nazar* in Arabic. It's an amulet to protect against *al-ayn*, the evil eye." If the amulet had fallen from this man, he wasn't Latino. His roots were in the Middle East.

4

When school consolidation swept the county in the 1980s, leaving the high school and junior high side-by-side in the middle of a cornfield far enough from any town that none could claim them as their own, the Crayton city hall and police station moved into the abandoned high school two blocks off the square. The sheriff's department waited another decade until banks began to gobble each other up, then relocated to the old bank building when it was replaced by a branch of First Ozark out on the highway.

I was three years old at the time, riding into town on weekends on my mother's lap in an old F-150 pickup that's still in a little barn behind the house. So, I didn't exactly have any say in the department's move. But I've thought since that we got the better end of the deal. The old bank faces the courthouse across Adams, a short walk to pick up a county record or escort a prisoner to a hearing. What was once the vault has become a perfect evidence room, already supplied with metal shelving and secure lockboxes. Two back offices, intentionally built with thick, reinforced concrete walls and no windows, made a perfect jail. The one not-so-grand part of the move from a drafty metal building on the north edge of town was that the sheriff got the loan officer's glass-sided cubicle as his office. We call it the fishbowl. It may have been a smart thing to be able to keep an eye on loan officers while they met with prospective borrowers. But it's not always helpful to see who's meeting with the sheriff. The temporary solution was pull-down accordion shades that soon became permanent, giving the impression something secret and sinister must be going on behind those blinds. I keep them raised unless something secret and sinister *is* going on.

Bobby Lule had stayed out at the site of the explosion until his shift ended at 8:00. The three day-deputies crowded into the fishbowl: Grace seated in her favorite corner chair where the window walls come together, Rocky D'Amico perched loosely on a folding chair in front of the desk, and Frankie leaning nervously against the doorframe. The shades were down.

We call Rocky our Jail Commander, charging him with keeping an eye on the rare prisoner we get, watching over the evidence room, and cruising the areas just beyond the city limits every few hours to show some presence of law and order. He's in his late fifties, about sixty pounds on the heavy side, and as friendly as Fred Rogers. People around Crayton love him, but he's slow on the hoof and a heart attack waiting to happen. I try to leave Rocky within spitting distance of the office.

Frankie's a man who doesn't sit easily. He's thin, wiry, and weasel-eyed, with a pencil-thin mustache he constantly smooths with a thumb and index finger. Frankie's in constant motion, bouncing a foot and nodding his head even when he's supposed to be standing still. Though he's never actually shot anyone, Grace is so convinced that he wants to that she refuses to back him up on a call when it looks like there might be any chance of gunplay. He was first to speak when we finally settled into the shrouded office.

"So, are you thinking what I'm thinking, Tate?" he asked, shifting nervously against the doorframe. Everyone in the county calls me Tate, even when we're talking official business. I tried for a few months to get them to call me Sheriff, but gave up when Marti, who's been the office assistant through three generations of sheriffs and three times as many deputies, reminded me that my predecessor had so sullied the title that people preferred to use something else. Plus, the Tate name carries some intimidation value in the county. All the Tates anyone can remember were a tough, ornery bunch who didn't back away from a brawl and usually came away as the last men standing.

I kicked back in my swivel chair behind the desk and propped a legal pad on one knee. "Depends on what you're thinking, Frankie.

Are we talking about the body, or the dam being blown up?"

The deputy shrugged loosely. "Could be both, I guess. But I was thinking mainly about the dam."

"The Greaves?" Grace guessed for the rest of us. "You're thinking the Greaves blew the thing up?"

"Damn right," Frankie nodded. I wondered fleetingly if anyone else was getting a chuckle out of all the unintended "dam" puns, but quickly let it go. I was the only one in the room who'd grown up fascinated by words and the mystery of different languages. I wasn't the finest torchbearer for the old Tate mystique.

"They've refused to move out of the holler and won't take the money that's been offered 'em," Frankie argued. "Have a suit against the water company and claim their land is sovereign territory. Not subject to the laws of the county or of the U.S. of A. We've been told that if they don't move, when they get ready to flood the valley we're going to have to go haul them out. Ain't somethin' I'm looking forward to, and I'd stake my reputation as a lawman that it was the Greaves blew up the dam."

Grace and I avoided exchanging a quick glance, not wanting to risk an involuntary smirk. We both knew the other was thinking the same thing. Frankie's reputation wasn't much of a wager. Barney Fife putting his good name on the line. But we had also both reached the same conclusion. Everyone living in Blackjack Holler has been mad as hell about the eminent domain landgrab. A few half-heartedly fought back. But everyone except the Greaves eventually settled. The belligerent father and son continued to defy both the water company and the law. I'd pretty well reconciled myself to the fact that within a few months, we were going to have to go drag them out, surrounded by heavy backup.

"It would have been Verl," Grace observed from her corner. "I hear LJ's never really recovered from being shot by your state trooper friend. He's pretty much confined to a chair."

By "your state trooper friend," Grace was talking to me. And she meant Officer Mara Joseph. The state investigator had left a 9 mm round in LJ Greaves' side when he pulled a shotgun on her during a murder investigation. The Greaves hadn't been the killers, but decided their sovereignty was being violated when we went into the holler to question them about who might have suffocated the old woman who lived on the adjoining property. I had to agree with Frankie. Going back wasn't something I looked forward to.

I jotted the Greaves names on my pad. "Whoever did it used something pretty powerful. It took more than a few sticks of dynamite to create that crater and throw the body that far."

"We found quite an arsenal in that rathole of a building they call home," Grace noted. She had joined a team from the state patrol that had searched the corrugated barn the men live in after Joseph and I had found the place packed floor-to-ceiling with every imaginable piece of junk. Both entrances had been boobytrapped.

"All firearms," I reminded her. "No explosives."

Her shrug showed that she wasn't convinced. "We didn't get into those piles. Just emptied the cabinet that was beside the back door. Who knows what else they have hidden in there. And they're the kind of men who have connections to heavy stuff if they decided they need some."

"Well, you're likely to see Joseph again," I said, keeping my eyes away from Grace. "I called troop headquarters in Springfield on the way back into town and told them we'd need help with this one. We don't have the tools or manpower to do the kind of investigation this is going to take."

"Are they sending Joseph down?" Grace asked.

I tried to shrug in a way that said, "Don't know and don't care." Even though Grace lives off and on with Sal, when Mara Joseph helped with my first murder case as sheriff, there had been some visible tension around the office. I first attributed it to Grace resenting another strong-willed woman sticking her nose into our jurisdictional business. Marti hinted that maybe it was because Joseph is a pretty nice looking woman in her own right and the first I'd paid attention to since losing Adeena. When I'd asked

Marti why that should make any difference to Grace, she just gave me one of her "sometimes you can be such a knucklehead" looks.

"I'll take that 'don't know' as a 'yes,'" Grace muttered.

"Take it as an 'I don't have any idea,'" I corrected, which was true. "But we've got to have some state help. I seriously doubt that whoever buried our John Doe in the dam blew the thing up. They planted him there to keep the body from ever being discovered. So we've got two pretty heavy crimes on our hands. A major destruction of property case and a murder. I'm thinking of completely turning the dam explosion over to the state since it involves a public works project. We'll focus our attention on finding out who our victim is and who shot the man in the head."

"What was that evil eye thing all about?" Frankie asked, lifting his cap and scratching nervously at his thinning forehead.

"Common all over the Middle East and Asia," I said. "But I think that one was Mideastern. They call them the evil eye, but really carry them to ward off bad luck."

"Didn't seem to work for that guy," Rocky chuckled. "So you think he was probably from over there somewhere?"

The amulet was in a plastic evidence bag in the middle of the desk. I lifted it by the corner. "I don't think we can count on that. I used to carry one when I was in Iraq. I don't think I'm superstitious, but I figured every bit of luck would help."

"He wasn't from around here," Frankie insisted. "Even with the dirt all over him, I could tell he was someone I hadn't seen before."

Grace and I both nodded our agreement and I lowered the *nazar* back onto the desk. "We'll get some pictures from the crime lab when they get the body cleaned up and show them around. See if anyone recognizes the man."

In the outer office, we heard Bobby greet Marti and ask if we were holed away behind the shades. I waved to Frankie to invite him in. Bobby entered, took a quick look around to see who was present, then deposited a brown shoe beside the bagged charm.

"Found the other one," he said, stepping back to give the others a clear view of the evidence. "It was on the other side of the creek, about half the distance the body was from the crater. I figure the explosion blew the guy upward and maybe into a spin, throwing the shoe off in that direction."

Frankie shuffled nervously against the doorframe. "I didn't get to the other side of the creek with my searching," he muttered defensively. "Or I'd have found it."

I raised a hand to show it wasn't a big deal. "Someone found it, so that's good. Did you come up with anything else?" I asked Bobby.

"Not really. There was a lot of stream trash, and I flagged and recorded it all like Frankie was doing." Acknowledging Ritter's work took a little of the fidgeting out of the man. "But you might want to take a good look at that shoe, Tate. The inside of the tongue. It looks like it's got some writing on it you might be able to figure out."

I leaned forward, grasped the shoe's heel, and forced the tongue forward with a pen. A one-inch tag in tan cloth was stitched across the inside of the leather flap. For the first time in the year and a half I'd served as sheriff, my time as a Marine and government interpreter was about to pay off.

Bobby leaned forward over the desk. "I-raqi writing, isn't it?" He'd seen enough signs and graffiti in Arabic, Farsi, and Kurdish while tromping through Iraqi villages to tie the squiggles and dots to the country.

"Close," I agreed. "But this is Syrian Arabic. It says, 'Made in Idlib.' That mean anything to anybody?" I glanced quickly around the room into three blank faces.

"Idlib's in northwest Syria. Both a town and a province. It's been one of the last rebel strongholds. How about Khan Shaykhun? Does that ring a bell?"

More blank stares.

"How about sarin gas?" All four heads nodded.

"Well, the town of Khan Shaykhun is just south of the city of Idlib in the same province. That's where the biggest gas attack happened that you all heard about."

"The guy *did* look kind of like he might be an A-rab," Frankie muttered. "But what would a man from Syria be doing in our county—and buried out at the dam?"

"Maybe more than we'd like to know," I muttered. "You know the three refugee families that were taken in by the First Christian Church? The ones I help with teacher conferences?"

Again, all four heads nodded, a glimmer of understanding starting to show in Grace's dark eyes.

"Well," I said, pushing back from the desk. "All three of those families come from Ariha. That's in the province of Idlib."

5

My phone buzzed as Grace and I were leaving the office for the Haddad home. The number was still in my directory from six months ago.

"Well, Officer Joseph," I answered, glancing over at Grace whose jaw tightened visibly. "Have you been assigned to our bombing?"

"That, and to help you with your murder. In fact, I have some morgue photos with me that will give you a clearer image of your victim."

It was mid-afternoon. We'd spent the day filing reports, cataloging what evidence we'd been able to gather from the bomb site, and cleaning up a couple of minor complaints that still deserved attention. I'd been about to open the street door for Grace but waved her back into the office.

"How far out are you?" I asked Joseph. "We're on our way to see a family who might be able to connect some of the dots for us on this. But the photos will be helpful."

"About ten minutes. Can I meet you somewhere?"

I shook my head, more for Grace's benefit than for the voice that couldn't see me. "These are recent immigrant families that still aren't too trusting of authority, especially police. I do some interpreting for them and know them well. We need to make this a local visit."

"Whatever you say. I'll bring the photos by the office, then drive on out to the dam."

I glanced at the wall clock behind Marti's desk. It was just after 4:00. The Haddad men wouldn't be off work for half an hour, and a visit to the families without the men present would be both inappropriate and resented. And it probably wouldn't tell us what we needed to know.

"Great. We'll wait until you get here." I hit the disconnect and steered Grace back toward the fishbowl.

"Was that your friend, Officer Joseph?" Marti asked from her desk, keeping her eyes mainly on Grace.

I stopped in the middle of the outer office, looking from one to the other. "What's with this 'Your friend Joseph?' Yes. She's been sent down by the Patrol and will be helping with the investigation. But I haven't seen her in six months." Which was true—but not because I hadn't tried.

I'd once commented that when on the job, Mara Joseph was like a hunting bobcat: sleek, compact, intense, and fearless. But while we had worked together to investigate the death of Nettie Suskey, my first murder as the new sheriff, I'd come to know the warmer, more sensitive side of this pretty, petite St. Louis transplant. We'd sparred a little about her being from an established Jewish family while I'd spent all of my adult life studying Arabic and Farsi and had been engaged to a Palestinian. But she understood the indiscriminate tragedy of the Middle East conflict that had taken Adeena's life when a hotel in Baghdad where she was interpreting was bombed by Al Qaeda. Joseph had also experienced some of the fragility created by deep personal loss, and we had found solace in each other's company. One of those times of solace, known only to me and Joseph as far as I knew, had ended in an exhausting, but completely sensational night together—at least for me. I'd tried to encourage a relationship after the case ended, but she hadn't been ready to jump back into the fire. We honestly *hadn't* spoken or seen each other in six months.

"My recollection," Marti said, refreshing our memories, "is that when she was here last, we didn't see much of you around the office—or get a lot of help with the routine little problems that all the rest of us were having to take care of."

I didn't try to argue the point. "That was then. This is now. She'll be working on the dam explosion. We'll concentrate on who put the body out there and why."

Marti lifted her nose with a dismissive sniff. "We'll see how that goes."

I again chose not to argue. Marti Bleasdale has been with the department since Christ was a baby and has more institutional memory than all of our bank of files combined. She has an irritating inclination to offer unsolicited advice and is overly protective of Grace, but that memory and uncanny intuition make it well worth keeping her around. The fact that she's discreet, completely loyal if you do your job, and knows more about what's going on in town than anyone but Jerry at Family Market makes her damn near indispensable. But she has a pain-in-the-ass habit of speaking truth when it's not wanted. As if to prove her point, as Marti returned to her typing, Mara Joseph pushed through the front door, nodded to the two women, and gave me a more than friendly smile.

"How you been, Tate? You're looking good."

She was dressed as she always does on the job: pressed jeans and a khaki shirt under an official patrol jacket. She looked every bit as good as I remembered.

"And you as well," I said, trying to sound welcoming rather than approving. I could tell from Marti's tight-lipped glance that it hadn't worked. I nodded toward Grace. "Why don't the three of us go into the office? Let's see what you have for us."

As had become the custom when Joseph helped with the Suskey case, she took Grace's favorite chair in the corner. The chief deputy propped herself beside the door. Joseph pulled a legal-sized envelope from an inside pocket of her jacket, drew out a photograph and card with two sets of prints, and tossed them on the desk. Grace stepped over to study them and Joseph scooted her chair closer to the desk. She tapped on the photo.

"Here's a shot of the man's face after the morgue got him cleaned up. And here are his prints. Both hands. We ran them through both state and federal databanks and came up empty. The lab's processing a DNA sample to see if he has one on file somewhere or if it links him to someone else we know of—and to try to get some kind of national or ethnic profile."

"He's Syrian," I told her. "From around the city of Idlib."

She arched a neatly shaped brow. "And you know this because—?"

I told her about the label in the stray shoe.

Joseph grinned. "I have a label in my shirt that says it's made in Vietnam. That doesn't mean I'm from Hanoi."

The plastic bag with the *nazar* still sat in the middle of the desk. I slid it over beside the photo. "Grace found this on the ground close to the body. It's a common Middle Eastern amulet that's supposed to ward off the evil eye. And Idlib isn't exactly a major exporter of shoes. I'd guess there are only one or two shoemakers in the city. And they probably have all the work they can do to keep up with local demand. Pretty sure this man bought his shoes in northwest Syria."

Joseph stood beside Grace, picking up the *nazar* and turning the bag in her hands. "I've seen these things. Usually as a necklace. Do you think the man was carrying it? If there was nothing in his pockets, I can't see a killer leaving that kind of evidence on a body."

"I suspect whoever killed the man didn't think the body would be found," Grace observed.

"Then why remove other identifying information?" Joseph argued. "No wallet or cards. No keys."

"Maybe the man wasn't carrying anything else for just that reason," Grace countered. "If he was picked up or killed, he didn't want to be identified. You said he didn't have prints on record. That's getting to be pretty unusual." The women had been in the same room for less than ten minutes and the air was already beginning to crackle.

Looking at the two standing beside each other across the desk, I couldn't help but be struck by the contrast: the lithe, gymnast-sized investigator with short, chestnut hair and a pixie-pretty face; Grace, a head taller with dark, expressive eyes and ebony hair that hung in a ponytail through the back of her cap to the middle of her back. I was tempted to let the debate continue, just to see how this would play out. But we didn't need tension on the team this early in the investigation.

"We'll run prints on the amulet and see what shows up," I interrupted. "If it belongs to the victim, my guess is that his will be all over it. If it's clean, it was probably planted. Or it could have just been dropped by somebody hiking along the creek. Since you're headed out to the bomb site, Joseph, you can help us by asking the construction people how someone was able to bury a body in the dam without being discovered. If whoever did it used earthmoving equipment, I'd think they would have been heard. And the soil around here is so rocky, you couldn't dig in it without using a pick or bar of some kind."

"Unless you were part of the crew," Joseph said. "I've got some people coming down to check for residue so we can identify the explosive. I'm going to begin by backgrounding everyone at the site. This strikes me as the kind of thing that might have been done by one of the workmen."

Grace saw another opportunity to contradict. "More likely by your friends, the Greaves. They're still holding out on selling their land and have a suit against Mid-Missouri Water."

Joseph looked at me sharply. "This true, Tate? The Greaves may be in the middle of this?"

I couldn't suppress a chuckle. "Might be. You'll probably need to go back down into the holler and confront the two of them. But it may just be Verl. LJ's still pretty stoved up from when you shot him." I winked at Grace. "To be safe, I think I'd take a couple of patrolmen down there with you."

"Not funny," Joseph grumbled. "That S-O-B turned a shotgun on me."

"You were on sovereign land," I grinned. "Just like you will be this time."

"We had reason to believe they were harvesting trees off Nettie's property," she insisted. "They looked like prime suspects."

"And they do again. But you know the Greaves. Not a spit of human kindness between the two of them." It was a description given by one of their neighbors that I knew Joseph would remember. "And you said you hoped you could nail them for something sometime. This might be your chance."

Joseph dropped the amulet back on the desktop. "I think I'll do the site investigation first. Maybe something will point in a different direction and I won't have to deal with the Greaves. What are you two up to today?" She said it more to Grace than to me.

Grace turned back toward the door, leaving me to answer. "There's a link here that has to be more than coincidental. We have three Syrian refugee families living in town, sponsored by the First Christian Church."

"Let me guess," Joseph said, smiling thinly and also turning toward the door. "They're from Idlib."

6

To give the Haddad men a little extra time to get home and settled in, I decided to start with the church pastor rather than the Syrian families. When we talked to the Haddads, we needed to have as much information as we could about how they ended up in Crayton, Missouri. Matt Frazee is a big man, about an inch shorter than I am at 6'2", and a good thirty pounds heavier. He looks more the medieval friar than twenty-first century pastor, with a cropped fringe around a balding head and short tawny beard. He's a bit of a free thinker theologically, and we have morning coffee together about once a month to argue the finer points of religion. He classifies himself as Christian, mind you, but is open to the idea that there are a number of pathways to God. Since Adeena's death, he's been one of the few people I can talk to who's willing to accept that her Muslim upbringing didn't automatically consign her to one of Dante's circles of hell. He's also quite the banjo player and is willing to give a hack picker like me a free lesson every now and then. We found him troubling over a sermon in the parsonage study.

He stood and clasped one of my hands and an elbow with a ministerial grip. "Good timing, Tate," he said, giving Grace a much more genteel handshake. "I've decided this Sunday I need to take on the problematic John 3:5. Frankly, I don't know exactly where to go with it."

One of the certainties of growing up in this part of the Bible Belt is that, as soon as a kid is old enough to listen to stories, he starts getting schooled in lessons from the Good Book. For me, that meant daily readings at home, weekly lessons at Sunday school, and scripture bees at church socials. Two of the ways I'd separated myself during childhood from the rest of the Tates of

Huckleberry Ridge were by being generally law-abiding and an obsessive bookworm. The inclination toward words and language favored me in the scripture competitions, and I could still retrieve good sections of the Old and New Testaments from memory. It was a talent that both impressed and frustrated Matt Frazee. Mother was a King James Bible devotee, so my memory was laced with the "thees" and "thous" of the 1611 translation.

"Baptism," I said. "'Except a man be born of water and of the Spirit, . . . ' yadda, yadda."

Matt chuckled. "Very good, Tate." He glanced at Grace to see if she might tolerate a little theology before we got down to business. Her amused smile gave him what permission he needed. "So, given your concern about your friend Adeena, what do you make of that passage?"

Matt knew Adeena had been a Palestinian transplant to Chicago and the daughter of a devout Muslim family. Though not practicing, she still thought of herself as Muslim. I'd used my Matt discussions to muddle through the worries about her death that lingered from my own fire and brimstone upbringing—so far, without resolution.

I glanced apologetically at Grace and frowned cynically. "Most around here would see that as meaning baptism and confirmation are essential to salvation."

Matt nodded. "But . . . ?" he urged.

"But, I've heard it explained as meaning we need both a temporal birth—being born of the water, like out of amniotic fluid—and then needing some kind of spiritual birth, as through grace or something similar." I winked at Grace who rolled her eyes.

Matt's brow knitted thoughtfully. "And what do *you* think?"

I shrugged, not sure it was a good idea to pursue this line too much farther with my devout Catholic deputy listening in. But I couldn't resist throwing out another idea.

"The early Christian Gnostics would probably have argued that baptism wasn't needed at all, because the Spirit of God already exists within us all and simply needs to be discovered."

"*Hah*! You really *are* a heretic, Tate," the reverend said with a low chuckle. "But I'm not sure I'm ready to bring the Gnostics into a sermon. We're a liberal congregation, but probably not that liberal."

I gave him a tilt of the head. "You brought it up. You have the most open group of followers in Crayton, Matt. If anyone will listen without running you out of town on a rail, your people will."

"But we're still not open enough to draw you back into the fold, Tate," he chided. That was my signal to get back to business. I gave him a brush-off smile and glanced again at Grace who was staring at me with a "Where does all of that useless stuff *come* from?" expression. Matt guided us to a sofa along one wall of the study.

"I really came to ask what you could tell me about the Syrian families," I said, shifting gears.

He glanced sharply from me to Grace, then back to me. "Is there some kind of trouble?"

"No. But we're investigating a case that by some strange twist involves the Syrian city of Idlib. If I remember right, the Haddads come from near there."

Matt nodded, frowning suspiciously.

"Can you tell me how these three families happened to end up in Crayton? We're not exactly the first place a relocation agency would think of."

The pastor shrugged as if there weren't much to tell. "We talked as a church council, decided that as a community of faith we'd like to sponsor some refugees, and submitted an application to AIRS: the American Immigrant Relocation Service. They're a non-profit group that works with church organizations around the country. Our thinking was that it would be good for our congregation, for the community, and of course for the families we sponsored."

I nodded. So far, all three seemed to have been true. "Any idea how these particular families were chosen?"

"No. I know AIRS works with immigrants from all over. We were asked if we'd be willing to sponsor three Syrian Christian families. They were our first offer, and we accepted immediately."

"Was there ever any discussion about why these families should be placed in a small rural town in the middle of the country?"

Matt shook his head. "I've been told the family name means something like 'blacksmith,' though I guess you'd know that. These men aren't blacksmiths, but all three were welders and metalworkers before they came here. All very skilled. Kilgore Homes was willing to give them all jobs right away. I think that sealed the deal."

"How well do you know the families?"

"As well as any members of our congregation. Better than some. The wives are still unwilling to speak much. Their English was pretty poor when they came, and they don't work as hard as the men and children do to improve. The men spoke some English, and it's become much better. The kids? You know them through your school interpreting work. Excellent English."

"Are you aware of them leaving any kind of trouble behind? Anything that might follow them?"

Matt sniffed. "You mean aside from a war that destroyed their town and killed half the people of Idlib, including a lot of relatives? And I'm sure you know they came from an area where gas was used."

"Well, yes, I knew about that kind of trouble. I was thinking of something more personal that involved just these three families."

Matt had been leaning back in his swivel desk chair and tilted it forward, planting his elbows on the polished mahogany top. "What's going on here, Tate? Why these specific questions?"

I knew the pastor would honor a confidence. "I need you to keep this to yourself for now, if you would, Matt. Will you do that?"

He nodded. "Of course."

"The explosion last night? The one out at the new dam site on Mill Creek? It threw up a buried body. The damnedest thing is that from what we can tell, the man was Syrian—and from Idlib."

Matt slumped back again in his chair. "That does remind me of something," he admitted. "When I got back in touch with AIRS after learning who'd been assigned to us, I asked if they were sure the families would be okay with a fairly isolated community in middle America. The man laughed in a way I thought sounded kind of cynical."

"And did he say anything?" I pressed.

Matt steepled his hands, with his thumbs tucked under his chin. "He said, 'In this case, I think it might be exactly what they are looking for.'"

7

First Christian had purchased a dilapidated, repossessed fourplex on South Jefferson, given the new immigrant families a modest renovation budget, and turned the two-story apartments over to the Haddads to remodel. The families rented the fourth unit to a newly married couple in the congregation and, as a group, attacked the project with such fervor that the other rundown apartments on the other side of Jefferson had been forced to follow suit. Now both were considered reasonably habitable.

The oldest of the brothers, Yusef Haddad, had moved his family into the apartment on the lower right. As we approached the door, I gave Grace a quick lesson in Syrian hospitality.

"We will be welcomed even if they're just sitting down to dinner," I cautioned. "And probably invited to join them. If it isn't dinner time, they'll bring us tea and maybe some figs or dates and feel like we need to visit for a while about things in general before we get down to business. Let me take the lead on this."

"Maybe we can discuss baptism and the Gnostics," Grace suggested, refusing to let me know by her expression if she was teasing or being irritable.

I grinned over at her, deciding to assume teasing. "They're Syrian Christians, one of the oldest Christian sects in the world. They could probably tell us a lot about both. But I think I'll stick to how the men's jobs are, how the kids are doing in school, and what they hear from back home. That might give us a natural lead-in to asking if they know anything about this guy. Don't be surprised if his wife, Lilia, doesn't join us. And don't suggest that she should. Yusef will decide that."

Grace sniffed. "You're forgetting who you're talking to. I grew up in a home where my father decided everything. He still hasn't forgiven me for going to college and choosing law enforcement instead of getting married and having a houseful of kids." She pointed to a stylized, hand-shaped amulet that hung on the inside of the Haddad's doorframe, the palm displaying the cobalt eye in its center. "Look. Here's one of those symbols."

"It's a *hamsa*. The Syrian Christians call it the Hand of Mary," I explained. "To protect the house. It usually has that *nazar* in the middle of the palm."

Their son Samir, a senior at Crayton High, answered the door, smiled brightly, and invited us into a living room that immediately swept me back into the Middle East. Though the furnishings were loaners and hand-me-downs from church parishioners, the air smelled of lamb and eggplant, garlic, olive oil, and lemon. Otherwise plain walls displayed somber images of Jesus, Mary, and the Syriac saints. The one smiling photograph, centered over the sofa, was of a gray-bearded man in a black robe and hat the shape of an acorn cap. The Patriarch of Antioch. Three gold chains hung about the patriarch's neck, the central one holding an ornate crucifix, the others images of the Christ and Mother and Child.

"Father, it is Mr. Tate," the boy called. After a moment of muffled conversation in the rear of the apartment, Yusef Haddad emerged from a back room. He is a handsome man in his mid-forties with dark wavy hair streaked with silver that he combs back off a wide forehead. He has the solid, muscular frame of a metal worker, but the proud, upright bearing of a man who is comfortable with his role as head clansman. He studied his visitors with a fixed smile.

"Ah! Mr. Tate. Welcome to my home." As I introduced Grace, he bowed slightly, ran a critical eye over her uniform, but did not offer to shake hands.

"Come. Please be seated. Samir, tell your mother to bring tea and biscuits. We have honored guests."

Grace and I sat stiffly on the threadbare sofa, an appropriate distance apart. Yusef took a deep recliner.

"Is your family settling well?" I asked, forcing aside my American urge to get right to the point of the visit.

"Yes. Very well. And I am most grateful for the help you have given when Lilia and the other women meet with the children's teachers at school. I know the children speak English very well, but the women? Ah, they have been slow to learn, and the men are not always able to come. The mothers must be told what the teachers say by someone other than a child." His smile turned sly. "Sometimes a son or daughter may not want a mother to know everything. Your assistance has been such a blessing to us."

"And the children are all doing well at school?" I knew they were. I heard the reports as often as the parents did and understood from teachers' comments that failure was not an option among the Haddad children. All the Syrian kids were near the top of their classes. But we were still at the polite conversation stage.

"Yes. Samir is on the football team. Ah, no. I mean soccer." He chuckled. "I grew up with it as a boy, and to me, it is still football. Samir has been playing all his life and is one of the best."

"Yes. I've been told that by the coaches. And Miriam is a favorite of her teachers. She is very talented at mathematics."

Yusef Haddad smiled proudly. "We had a very good business in our home city. Making gates and window coverings out of iron. The children helped and learned to do numbers in their heads. Algebra was developed by the Arabs, you know."

I nodded my understanding, hiding a smile as I remembered all of the advancements in science and mathematics Adeena liked to attribute to her ancestry.

Grace sat patiently as we chatted about the Haddad's oldest daughter Raca's job at the Casey's General Store, and that Yusef had been persuaded to let her enroll in a nursing program at the community college. "I still do not like her driving to Springfield alone each day," he grumbled, the smile disappearing. "But everyone is trying to turn me into an American father."

"Are they succeeding?"

"I certainly hope not," he said without humor.

Raca appeared from the back of the apartment carrying a platter with a tea kettle, cups, a plate of dried figs, and what looked like shortbread cookies. She smiled an acknowledgement, looked admiringly at Grace, and poured us each tea without speaking. Yusef also shifted his gaze to Grace.

"You must be the deputy I have heard the men talk about at work." There was a note of disapproval in his voice. "The woman policeman in the town."

Grace's face turned a deeper shade of bronze, but she held the man's gaze. "I do my best to be a good officer," she said firmly.

Yusef nodded and again studied her with dark, critical eyes, then decided we had taken care of necessary formalities. "But you have come for some purpose," he said. "How may I help you?"

I waited until Raca had returned to the kitchen, then briefly described the explosion at the dam and discovery of the body. Yusef listened attentively, his face a relaxed mask. Samir had taken another overstuffed easy chair and leaned forward with fists locked under his chin, captivated by descriptions of explosions and bodies being thrown into trees.

"We have come to see you, Yusef, because there was a label in the man's clothing. In one of his shoes. It showed it to have come from Idlib."

The calm on the man's face disappeared in an instant, replaced by a focused intensity that told me the casual comment to Matt Frazee by the AIRS relocation worker had carried much more importance than the pastor realized. The Haddads had come here seeking remote isolation for a reason. Yusef recovered as quickly as the mask had crumbled.

"That is indeed a coincidence," he said calmly. "What do you know about this man?" Lilia Haddad had returned with the kettle to refill our cups and paused beside her husband to listen.

"Nothing, really. I have a photo—but it's not a pleasant sight." I glanced over at Samir who had become even more intrigued.

Yusef waved away my concern. "We have all seen more death than anyone should endure in a lifetime. Let me see your photograph."

I drew out the picture and laid it on the table in front of him. Yusef had prepared himself and his expression remained unchanged. But Lilia tried unsuccessfully to smother a loud gasp with her free hand. Samir looked up at his father with undisguised alarm.

"They have found us," Lilia murmured in Arabic, forgetting for the moment that I understood every word. "The old women saw this. Death has come. And it is close to us."

Yusef replied gruffly in Arabic, waving to indicate that his son should follow his wife from the room. When we were alone, he pushed the photo back across the table, smiling thinly. "Had you not seen the reaction of my family, perhaps I would have attempted a lie. They have forced me to be my better self and be truthful with you."

I tucked the picture back into an inside pocket. "I see that you recognize the man. What did your wife mean? 'They have found us?' And about the old women seeing this?"

The Syrian planted his hands on his knees, his jaw tightening. "We left a country at war," he said grimly. "Idlib was one of the last centers of resistance. But even within the city, there were divisions. We had enemies. This man was one of them."

"An enemy who would pursue you here?" Grace asked.

Yusef sniffed dismissively. "You do not understand our culture, Deputy. Even in wartime, the ancient demands of honor and revenge remain a family obligation."

I followed with the obvious question. "Why might this man be seeking revenge?"

Yusef had kept his dark eyes on Grace and quickly shifted them back to me with a cool gaze. "We were enemies. That was all the reason he needed."

Somehow that answer didn't explain a man hunting down a

family that had hidden in the Ozark hills half a world away. "I know the codes of honor," I said. "This man would not come here after you simply because you were his enemy."

"In a war, enemies kill enemies," he said curtly. "The Haddads killed some of this man's family."

"And what was the man's name?"

"Farid Sayegh."

"Had you or anyone in your family seen Farid here?"

Yusef's gaze hardened. "You saw my wife's surprise. Did it appear the reaction of someone who knew he was here?"

"It may have been a surprise to your wife, but not to everyone."

"No one in my family knew he was here," Yusef said firmly.

"What did your wife mean by 'The old women saw this?'"

Yusef called back into the kitchen for Raca and Lilia. Lilia was still trembling when she entered the room, Raca holding her arm.

"What did you mean when you spoke of the old women?" Yusef demanded in Arabic.

Raca glanced apologetically at her mother, then answered for her in English. "Mother worries about her family still in Syria. We were told the old women who live on the mountain can see the future. I took mother to their home. They said they could see that there had been a death. Someone from our home—and that it was close."

Yusef spoke sharply in Arabic. "You have been to a fortuneteller?"

Lilia cowered behind her oldest daughter who straightened protectively. "You do not let us contact family. Mama worries about her family."

Yusef began to reply, but thought better of it with guests in the room.

Grace had pulled a notepad from her shirt pocket and spoke to Raca. "By 'old women,' do you mean the Webber sisters?"

Raca shook her head uncertainly. "I don't know their names. One of the women at the church English class mother goes to told her she should go see the 'Old Women of the Woods.' When I went to pick Mother up, the lady told me how to find them."

"Down in the corner of the county? A long hike up the hill to the house? The women are twins?" Grace asked.

The girl nodded. Grace jotted a note on her pad and glanced over to signal she had what she wanted. I turned again to Yusef who sat brooding in the stuffed chair.

"And your brothers?" I asked. "Neither of them was aware that this Farid Sayegh was in the area?"

"I do not speak for my brothers. But they would have told me."

"Do you know of anyone else who might want to kill Mr. Sayegh?"

The Syrian sneered. "I know hundreds who would like to kill him. But none are here."

I nodded as if this made sense. It also meant that the likely killers were here in this fourplex.

"It looks like the man died about three days ago. Can you account for your time on Tuesday and Wednesday?"

Yusef shrugged. "I worked. My brothers worked. We went to a church meeting on Wednesday night. Then I was at home. We do not go out."

"And your brothers? Other than work?"

"You must talk to them directly about the rest of their time. We all went to the church meeting. We are very grateful to this church. In the evenings, all the families come together after we eat. But we do not all sleep in the same house, so who can say for sure? But I know my brothers would not harm the man without my knowing."

I glanced over at Grace. "Any other questions from you, Officer Torres?"

"Yes. A couple. Was this Mr. Sayegh relocated at the same time you were, Mr. Haddad?"

Yusef grimaced and shook his head. "He was one of Assad's people. He would not have been taken in by the United States."

"So you are assuming he was not in this country legally."

"I am quite certain he was not."

"Do you believe he was here looking for you?"

Yusef raised his hands in a gesture of uncertainty. "Who can know such a thing? But he was here. This is not a town a man just drives through when he is touring in America for a few weeks. We are his enemies. What other conclusion can we make?"

Grace gave me another head nod to signal she had asked all her questions.

"I think that will be all for now, Mr. Haddad. Please excuse our intrusion on your family this evening. But please also ask your brothers if they know anything that might be helpful. Give me a call if they have information. I will probably be getting in touch with each of them, so tell them to expect a visit and stay in town." We all stood, and Yusef escorted us to the door.

"I shall speak to them. And I will surely call you if we have anything to say," he promised. He remained on the doorstep as we walked to the car, following us with a grim frown.

As we reached the car, my cell buzzed. It was Joseph.

"Are you where you can talk?" she asked when I answered.

"Yes. We're just leaving the home of one of our Syrian families."

"Can you meet me at the office? I have some interesting information about the bombing here and thought you might want to drive up to Springfield with me."

"Oh? What's up?"

Grace was watching me closely.

"When you said you thought the body you found was Syrian, we mailed the morgue photo to Washington," Joseph said. "They're flying someone out. I'm headed to the airport to pick up a guy from the FBI's counterterrorism division. I thought you might want to be there to meet him with me."

8

"What was that all about?" Grace asked as we left the Haddad home. "I thought we were taking the murder case, and State was checking out the explosion at the dam."

"It looks like the Feds are coming in. And I got the impression Officer Joseph thinks the two might be related."

Grace sniffed under her breath but said nothing. I decided it might be wisest to leave Joseph out of the conversation for now and let her fill us in when we reached the office. "What did you make of what Yusef had to say?" I asked.

"It's got to be a lot more than coincidence that this guy shows up here and was a known enemy of the family in Syria. Mrs. Haddad—Lilia, or whatever her name is—seemed really terrified. The father? I'm not so sure. I can't say that I like the man. He's too much like some others I know. But they must have put those families here because they suspected someone might come looking for them and felt like they'd be hard to find here. The FBI sending someone in from Washington would support that."

"Sounds right to me," I agreed. "And I don't like what it suggests. If Washington didn't know the guy was in the country until the state patrol sent the photo, that makes me think someone here killed him. Someone who knew about the water project and figured if they buried him in the dam, he'd never be found."

"Wouldn't that mean that whoever blew up the dam wasn't connected in some way to the murder?" Grace objected. "The killer would want the body to stay covered up."

"Unless that someone wanted the body found to implicate our Syrians. They'd know that sooner or later we'd tie the victim back to the Haddads."

Grace shook her head. "So someone knew the Haddads had

killed the guy and buried him in the dam, then blew him back out? Not likely, I think." She paused, then added, "Unless this Farid wasn't here by himself."

My turn to shake off her suggestion. "If there was someone else, I think they'd just go after the families again. Why go to all the trouble to blow the dam up and make us piece all this together?"

"To let us take care of the Haddads for them," she suggested.

I wasn't convinced. "I don't think that's the kind of revenge they'd be after. They'd want blood."

"This revenge thing," Grace wondered. "It's really that deeply imbedded in the culture?"

"It is. Sort of like the old Hatfields and McCoys. You kill one of ours. We have to kill one of yours."

"If this guy had gotten to one of the Haddads, would the families here feel like they needed to go back and revenge the killing?"

I chuckled cynically. "You saw Yusef. I guess it depends on how much of an American father he's become."

"Was he telling us the truth about the family not knowing Sayegh was here?"

"You never can be sure. You might have noticed he was quite careful not to say that *he* didn't know Farid was here. He just said the family didn't know. But if I had to bet on it, I'd say he was telling the truth. And I don't think the brothers would kill the man without letting him know."

We rode in silence until back on the square. I parked in front of the building we jokingly call the Blockhouse because of the solid old limestone construction and a single window looking out from what had once been the lobby. No other natural light. Joseph's car wasn't in one of the reserved spots.

"What do you think about the visit to the Webber sisters?" Grace wondered, wanting to talk this through before Joseph was part of the discussion.

I raised my hands in surrender. "I've quit trying to figure those two ladies out. They've been reading tea leaves since I was a kid. My mother used to swear by them, and half the people in town still go out there sometimes. I think even Reverend Latimer's wife gets readings every now and then. Jerry takes groceries up to them every week. A couple of years ago, they told him he should call me before he left to come back into town—to let me know he was going to be in an accident and would need some help. He didn't call because he didn't believe the old ladies. A deer ran in front of him and he swerved off the road into a tree. Knocked him out cold. Lucky for him, someone else came by and saw the car."

"So, you believe in them?"

"Let's just say I can't explain them."

"Will it do any good to go talk to them?"

I looked over with a grin and pushed open the car door as Officer Joseph pulled up beside us. "I was just going to suggest that you run out there tomorrow. Let's see what Joseph has to say. Then maybe you can fill in the gaps with a reading."

Mara Joseph held out a three-inch length of black insulated wire with a small clip on one end. "Recognize this?" she asked.

I did. "Looks like the detonation cord from an M183."

"Very good. And there's C4 residue all over that site out there. Someone blew up the dam using a military demolition kit, placed about in the center of the concrete culvert that's handling the water from the stream while the dam's being constructed. The blast throwing up a slab of concrete was probably what kept the body above it from being blown to pieces."

"Someone obviously knew what they were doing."

"Or didn't know there was a body there, and it just happened that way. Do your Syrians have military experience?"

"They were resistance fighters," I told her. "But I don't know what that means in terms of formal military training. Especially with explosives. We did learn that they knew the man. And that there was some kind of bad blood between the families. I think it's pretty likely he was here on some kind of vendetta mission."

"All the more reason to suspect them of both," Joseph said. "They are the only ones who would have recognized the man, and they knew about the dam construction."

I shook my head. "You don't just run over to Home Depot and buy an M183 kit. I don't know where they'd get anything like that, and neither would they. And as Grace said as we were driving back, why would they kill someone, bury the body, and then blow it back out of the ground?"

"I have a theory about that," Joseph said. Grace raised a cynical brow and rolled her eyes. Joseph missed the display.

"After they planted the body, they decided they needed to send a message back to whoever sent this guy. Let them know he hadn't succeeded in getting the job done."

"No, no," I muttered dismissively. "Two problems with that. Maybe three. First, that's a pretty extreme way to expose the body again. Why not just go back out there, dig him up, and leave him in the woods somewhere? Plus, why draw all that extra attention to an investigation? We're now not only investigating a murder, but checking to see who was able to get a military demolition pack and blow up a public works project. Double exposure."

Joseph wagged her head, thinking that over. "Okay. That's two reasons. What's the third?"

"If this guy was coming after them, I'm not sure they would want to get word back to whoever sent him that he'd failed. I'd think that might add to the vendetta. They'd be better off to just let him disappear."

Grace jumped into the conversation from the chair in the corner, which she'd managed this time to commandeer before Joseph could get seated. "We seem to be making a lot of assumptions here. First of all, aside from knowing these Syrians knew each other and had some bad war history, nothing else ties the Syrians to the murder. When we met with them, I think they were genuinely surprised to learn about the guy being here. And nothing really ties the explosion to the body. We know a bunch of people are upset about that dam, and the Greaves are as likely to be able to get C4 as anyone around here. They're linked to all those white nationalist groups. And they have a lot more reason to want the dam gone than the Haddad families. I think we need to slow down and start doing some basic police work."

She was right, of course. Joseph's dark look showed she knew it too and didn't like being lectured on basic procedure. But the FBI wasn't sending a counterterrorism guy out here for the hell of it. And what were the odds of two enemies from a small city in northwest Syria showing up in an even smaller town in the Missouri Ozarks by accident? Slim to none. The Haddads had to be involved somehow.

"Let's go see what our man from Washington can tell us," I suggested, pushing out of my chair. "And Grace, when you go see the Webber sisters in the morning, have them look at the leaves and see if they can tell us who killed Farid Sayegh."

9

Joseph drove her state Tahoe, believing for some reason that it would be more appropriate for a state investigator rather than a county sheriff to meet the guy from Washington. I disagreed, as much because of my general distaste for the hierarchies that exist in law enforcement as for my feeling that this was my case. He should have to be dealing with me. But it was one of those issues that didn't merit getting my britches in a knot, so I chose not to argue the point. Plus, it gave me a chance to guide the conversation from the passenger seat.

"Did you ever manage to get back to Mazatlán?" I asked after we cleared town and seemed on neutral ground. We had spent two days in the Mexican city on the Nettie Suskey murder case, tracking down a dealer in Civil War era American gold coins. The time together had kindled a spark I thought might turn into a relationship. But Joseph had decided she didn't want to get that close, still smarting from having let that happen with an earlier partner, with bad results. But by the time the case ended, she was hinting that she would enjoy spending a week getting to know the Mexican city better and might enjoy company. I had spoken to her three times since, all within a month of wrapping up the case. But no invitation to return to Mazatlán.

She looked over, smiling thinly. "No. Didn't ever go back. Thought about it a few times, but either didn't want to take the time off, or wasn't sure I wanted to risk getting back together."

"Is that the same reason all my dinner invitations needed a rain check?"

"I think you only called three times."

"Yup. Only three. It would have been a lot simpler if you'd just said, 'Enough already! I don't want us to get back together.'"

"I wasn't sure I didn't. I just couldn't get myself to recommit. Plus, I could see how badly Grace wanted to be in that role in your life. And you weren't entirely disinterested in her."

"I told you before that Grace has a serious boyfriend. And we work too closely together to get involved. You know the problems that can cause."

Her smile turned cynical. "And you don't see *this* as working too closely?"

"This is what? A case every six or eight months that might bring you down our way? Once a year? That's hardly bedfellows."

She nodded grimly. "I know you're right. And I have to admit, I felt a real surge when the division commander called to tell me you needed some state assistance again. I'd been wanting an excuse to see you, Tate. I just didn't want to initiate it."

"Well, here we are. Do you think we might be able to work dinner into some evening this week?"

"Let's see where this goes with the FBI man. Our evenings might be pretty full."

I can be slow. I mean, the second dinner turn-down should have been enough. But this time, I knew a "back off" when it came my way. I changed the subject. "So, what are you expecting from this guy? Did the Bureau say any more than that he was coming?"

She relaxed a little. "Nothing but that he's from counter-terrorism. I take that to mean they recognized our man and he's on one of their lists."

"Did you have time before you came down to run his name through the databases you have access to?"

"I did. Came up empty. The Bureau sends us lists of people they have a special interest in. He wasn't on any of them. What did your families tell you?"

"They were on different sides of the Syrian civil war. Idlib has been at the center of final efforts by the Assad government to crush the rebels. Our dead man supported Assad, and the Haddads the rebel group. There was some killing that involved the families.

That's about all I could get from them."

"Not much justification for sending someone halfway around the world to seek revenge."

I chuckled. "One of the first lessons I learned when I was deployed to Iraq was that nothing is ever as simple as it seems in that part of the world."

"Or in this part," she offered.

I don't remember ever having met an FBI agent in person. I'd worked with DOD intelligence officers in Iraq. And some people I suspected were CIA. But never an FBI agent. Special Agent Warren Rosario didn't disappoint. He was taller than average, maybe 6' 1" or 6' 2", with a military haircut, intense hazel eyes, and the requisite dark suit and tie. I had started to have TV images of the FBI in jeans and blue vests with "FBI" emblazoned in bold letters across the back. It was good to see that the old Hoover influence hadn't entirely been erased.

We shook hands all around, and I dutifully grabbed his roller bag.

"Anyone from your local office meeting you?" Joseph asked.

Rosario grinned. "They don't have any idea I'm here. Counterterrorism is something of its own master, and we don't always bring the local office in. We'd just as soon this situation be below the radar for now. When local agents get involved, so does the press."

"The dam explosion's made the papers," she told him. "But so far, we've been able to keep discovery of the body quiet."

"The construction people aren't talking?"

"They don't like the idea of a body being hidden in their dam any more than we do. And the night watchman's hanging onto his job on the condition he keeps his mouth shut. So far, no leaks."

Rosario seemed to want to talk about other things. "I think there must be a Springfield in every state," he joked as we walked to the Enterprise rental counter. "I almost boarded a plane to Illinois."

"It's happened," Joseph granted. "Have you reserved a place to stay?"

The special agent gave me a sidelong grin. "I looked for places near your little town, Sheriff, and only came up with a Super 8. So I'm booked into the Holiday Inn Express down on Highway 60. It looked like a good jumping-off spot to head toward Crayton. I'm a pretty avid fisherman and was thinking while I was here, I might as well stop by the Bass Pro mothership. And I hear their aquarium and wildlife museum are first class. All work and no play, as they say."

Somehow that all seemed a little less Hoover but gave Agent Rosario a bit more humanity than I'd initially granted the man. We waited until he had his rental, then led him south to the hotel and got him checked in. He came back into the lobby dressed more like the TV agents: jeans and a long-sleeved shirt, but no blue vest. The breakfast area was empty. We found a corner table and caught him up on what we knew.

He nodded and laid the morgue shot of Farid Sayegh on the table. "I have to admit, this photo took us by surprise. We had no idea this guy was in the country. In fact, he'd been seen around Idlib as recently as two weeks ago."

I didn't try to hide my surprise. "You had someone watching him there?"

"Not us. And not him specifically. But military intelligence and the CIA are watching general activity in the area twenty-four seven. They keep an eye on all the major players. I looked into your background, Sheriff Tate. Decorated Marine. Squad interpreter in Iraq and Afghanistan. Language Services with the State Department after your discharge. Not exactly who I expected to find out here. But perfect for this case. What do you know about this area of Syria?"

I considered saying something about his "Not exactly who I'd expected to find out here" coastal stereotype, but thought better of it.

"Northwest part of the country," I said instead. "Central to much of the rebel resistance and to some of the worst atrocities, including the gas attacks. Turkish presence in the area now. Significant Christian population in that part of the country. That's what our refugee families are." Rosario arched his forehead. Maybe the "out here" people aren't as backward as he'd thought.

"Exactly right," he agreed with an amused grin. "I wish all of our agents were that well informed. Anyway, as a result, it's been one of the most divided areas in terms of allegiance. Since the uprising began, there have been almost constant battles for control of villages in the area: Salqin, Armanaz, Harem, Sarmin. For the first number of years, it seemed government forces were always a step ahead of the FSA—the Free Syrian Army. One of the senior FSA leaders was a man named Yusef Haddad. Ring a bell?"

Joseph and I exchanged glances. A new piece to our complicated puzzle—and a significant omission by Yusef during my interview.

"The FSA finally figured out that it had a mole," Rosario continued. "One of the prominent families in Idlib, a family of three brothers named Sayegh who had appeared to be solidly in the rebel camp, turned out to be feeding information to government intelligence. Yusef hunted down the oldest of the brothers, a man named Samir, and executed him. Not too long after that, the politics of the region became so complicated it was hard to tell who was who. We started to pull back and extracted Yusef and his brothers and their families with him. They were sent out here because we feared something like this might happen if they were found."

Joseph entered the conversation. "You didn't change their names?"

Rosario chuckled. "I don't know that part of the world as well as your colleague here. But the way I understand it, these are proud people with centuries of history. They'd rather be discovered than become someone else."

I nodded my agreement.

"Any idea how they were located?" Joseph asked.

The agent gave a quick, frustrated shake of the head. "The other thing they won't give up are family ties. There will be an uncle in Minneapolis. A cousin in Phoenix. They call each other. And the divisions in the Syrian community in the US are almost as sharp as in their home country. The Assad government has eyes everywhere. Some cousin talks at a gathering of friends. The wrong people are listening. All our efforts to hide the families go out the window."

"How do you think this Farid got into the country?" I asked. "From what Officer Joseph told me, your people didn't know he was here."

Rosario grunted. "I hate to admit it, but we had no idea. I'd guess Canada on a passport from one of the Caribbean islands. St. Kitts or Dominica. Once into Canada, getting into the US undetected is pretty simple. What looks like a legitimate passport under an assumed name. If that doesn't work, there are thousands of miles of unprotected border that are crisscrossed by logging roads and off-road trails."

Joseph looked at me questioningly. I shrugged. This was all news to me as well. "St. Kitts?" she asked. "How would someone like that get a passport from St. Kitts?"

Rosario smiled thinly. "For decades, when someone sells property down there, it can be with or without a passport. If you include a passport, which can cost hundreds of thousands of dollars, it allows you to boost the price of your land. It's a little device that's been used to pad the foreign accounts of island officials. Good deal for everyone, except us. Questionable foreign nationals who have money buy a passport or two, let the land sit idle or hire someone to manage it, and use the passports to travel unchallenged around the world. I've heard there's a pretty lively black market on the islands by people who sublet these homes or condos without the owners even knowing about it."

More pieces to the puzzle, but some that didn't help our local picture.

"Are you thinking the Haddads saw the guy and killed him before he got to them?" I asked.

Rosario shrugged. "They may have seen him. May have been tipped off and were waiting. They may not be involved at all. Do you know where Sayegh was staying?"

"We traced him to the Hampton. He was checked in under his own name which he also used to rent a car from Avis. He was seen around the hotel for a couple of days, then disappeared without checking out. He'd left the room and car on a card that was valid. When we took the car back, he still had three more days on the rental. If he was here after the Haddads, it appears he wasn't sure when he could get to them."

"I'll talk to the families," Rosario said. "But I don't expect to learn much more than you did. They're tight-lipped and afraid of nothing. But I may be able to get some feel for how much they knew about his being here, once I inform them we know about Yusef's role in killing Farid's brother."

One of Rosario's statements had caught my attention. "You say the Haddads may not have been involved at all . . . and you seem to accept that as being as likely as that they were. Farid Sayegh's death obviously wasn't an accident. Who else might have been involved?"

Rosario paused, his jaw tightening, studying first me, then Joseph. "Yes. A slip on my part," he finally admitted. "But since you're both pretty critical to this investigation, I'll share this with you. There are a dozen groups of families like the Haddads. People we brought out of Syria, Iraq, or Afghanistan for their own protection. People with very personal enemies. Some were local translators, doing what you did, Tate. Interpreting for American forces. Some were informants for us who were found out and we had to get them to safety. Others, like Yusef Haddad, were opposition leaders. Early in our relocation history, we lost a couple of people to just this kind of thing: vendetta killings. But in three cases more recently, we have been called in on killings like Sayegh's where a man who appears to be an assassin was intercepted and eliminated before he could get to his target."

I leaned back in my chair, studying the FBI man. "And you don't know who got to these men?"

He shook his head. "No idea. If we were pretty certain the Haddads did this, we would probably pull them out immediately and stick them somewhere else. But if someone is getting to vendetta killers before we even know they're in the country, we aren't sure we could put them anywhere safe enough that whoever is doing this doesn't know where they are. Plus, we hope each time this happens, something might lead us to whoever's doing it."

I pushed again forward, straightening in the chair. "Let me get this straight. You have three or four cases like this where someone coming into the country to attack one of our protected immigrants has been intercepted and killed. And before he gets to his target."

"Yes. Just like in this case."

"Could it be someone inside the Bureau?"

Rosario shook his head. "If it is, they know one hell of a lot more than any of the rest of us. They'd have to have some pretty sophisticated outside sources of information about the movement of these vendetta killers. We don't track terrorist or unfriendly activity outside of the US. Someone with that kind of intel would probably be involved inside the warring countries and be using their own people to intercept."

"Someone like Central Intelligence."

Rosario shrugged skeptically. "We asked. They say no."

"These killings must have been miles apart. Do you think it's the same person who's carrying them out?"

"Maybe not the same person. But the same people. Connected in some way."

"Why do you say that?"

Rosario pulled a smooth round amulet from his pocket. "Do you know what this is?"

Joseph and I exchanged another quick look, and I nodded grimly. Another piece of the puzzle dropped into place. "A *nazar*. The evil eye amulet."

The agent chuckled. "You're the only local lawman I've talked to who had any idea what this is. But I guess I shouldn't be surprised. Well, all of our intercepted assassins didn't have anything on their bodies that identified them. In fact, because you could read that shoe label, Sheriff, you were the only local people who tied their John Doe to the Middle East." He held up the amulet, turning the piercing blue eye slowly between his fingers. "But all of the intercepted killers had one of these in his pocket."

10

I turned the fishbowl over to Special Agent Rosario. Joseph also asked for a space, so we shared the desk set aside for our two night deputies. Joseph used the swivel chair while I worked from a fold-out. Our two night guys rarely come into the office. Larry Newby is a retired security guard from Jack Henry and Associates, a business financial software company up in Monett. Larry is about as reliable on the job as an old Swiss clock: steady, durable, and spot on when you need to check some fact with the man. But he likes to have his days at home. He finishes his shift at 4:00 a.m., sleeps until just after noon, then works in his garden or woodshop until he comes on duty again at 8:00 p.m. If I tried to move him to days, he'd be gone in a heartbeat. He spends all of his duty time in his patrol car, with maybe an hour at the desk if he has a report to write up. As long as we don't leave the desk cluttered, Larry is fine with giving up the space.

Bobby Lule usually dictates his reports into a little digital recorder he keeps in his cruiser and leaves them for Marti to type up. The night desk doesn't get much use.

I got to the office just after 7:00 the morning Rosario was expected in Crayton. Marti always has a complaint list waiting, and I was still smarting from her little quip about leaving the rest of the team to take care of all the routine stuff the last time Joseph worked with us. If I could check off a couple of items before the pair arrived from Springfield for our first scheduled team briefing at 11:00, I could quiet some of the office grumbling. Grace was spending the morning visiting the Webber sisters. Frankie would stay up north and patrol. Whatever catch-up work got done before 11:00 depended on me and Rocky. If it required much exertion, it would all be mine.

I hadn't even reached my new desk before Lule called.

"Tate, better hook the trailer to your Explorer and load up the Gator. And call Chase. We've got the damnedest thing up here I've ever seen." Given the fact that Bobby had done two tours in Iraq and been with me when we found the Syrian's body draped over the limb on Mill Creek, that sounded pretty ominous.

"Where are you, Bobby? And what's going on?"

"I'm about halfway between Tug Divine's place and Nick's Tap Room. Up off Old Quarry Road. You know that stretch of woods that Tug hikes through when he goes to the bar?" It was one of those questions you ask when you know the other person will understand exactly where you're talking about but needs some orienting. And Tug's hike to Nick's Tap Room every afternoon is as much a part of daily routine in Crayton as his old postal route used to be.

Tug had retired early from the postal service with a disability everyone in town knew was the government's way of saying he was getting too drunk to safely stagger from one house to the next. So they gave him just enough pension to move into a rundown mobile home on Morrison Branch, a spring-fed tributary of Mill Creek. The decrepit single-wide was a half-mile through a stand of Conservation-owned timber from the only bar in town, Nick's Tap Room. Nick's bills itself as a microbrewery that sells its own recipes and half-a-dozen others from around the region, plus a limited selection of the harder stuff. Every afternoon since he left the postal service, Tug has weaved his way through the woods for as many shots of Jack Daniels as he can talk Nick into dispensing. When Nick cuts him off or they lock the place up at midnight, it's back along the beaten path to sleep it off until his next trek to keep the DTs at bay.

"You know how when Tug gets wore out sometimes, trying to make his way home, he'll hole up in that hollowed out sycamore?" Bobby asked. Another question intended to orient me to the bit of local lore important to whatever had happened during the night.

"Yeah. I know the tree." It had been hit by lightning decades ago, had managed to survive the trauma, but had a burned-out burrow just above the roots. The warren was just big enough for a man to crawl into when he didn't think he could make the trailer before losing consciousness.

"Well, it looks like Tug climbed in there last night, was too cold to pass out, and thought he'd warm hisself up by using his lighter on a nest some critter was building in there. Caught the whole damn tree on fire."

It took a few seconds to process what Bobby was telling me. "Was Tug in there? Did he get out?"

"Nope. At least we think it's Tug. The Carlsons were driving up Old Quarry Road just about sun-up and saw a curl of smoke out in the woods. Called it in. By the time I got here, the tree was pretty well burned up. Nothing else around it caught fire. Just the old tree and what must be Tug. Too damn charred to tell for sure. I couldn't get my cruiser back in here, so had to hike in. You'll need to bring the Gator."

"On my way," I said, still struggling to get a picture of the funeral pyre. "I'll call Chase and have him bring the ambulance or hearse out. Is that tree closer to Nick's place or Tug's trailer?"

"I think it'll be easier to come in from Tug's end," Bobby said. "The old guy was only two hundred yards from being home."

I called Chase Backman, who was already at the funeral home, left a note on the desk for Marti, and drove the Explorer around to the back of the Blockhouse where we'd added a garage to hold the trailer and Gator. Not how I'd expected to begin my first day collaborating with the FBI.

Our first little roundtable gave Special Agent Rosario a good Ozark introduction to a couple of our more colorful citizens. As the four of us pulled chairs up around the desk in the fishbowl, the special agent looked from Joseph to Chief Deputy Torres, then over at me with a slight smile that said "This is a damn sight prettier company than I'm used to sitting down with." I nodded to acknowledge that I was indeed a fortunate member of the law enforcement community, then asked the team to give me a few minutes as Frankie Ritter came into the outer office. Frankie had taken over at Tug's place when Bobby's shift ended, letting me work on a couple of items on Marti's list: a pickup abandoned on the shoulder out near Crawford's Junction. Reports of a meth lab at the back of the Trammell farm. It turned out Buzz Trammell was cooking moonshine, which isn't an offense in the state as long as he doesn't try to sell it—which, of course, he swore he never would.

"Come on in here, Frankie," I called through the window I'd chosen to leave uncovered. Then, to the group gathered around my desk, "You'll find this an interesting little side story to our morning. I need Frankie to catch me up on it, if you don't mind." While Frankie deposited some folders on Marti's desk and took a quick side trip to the head, I told them about Tug's suspected incineration. Frankie made it into the office to fill in the details.

"It was Tug, alright," he announced. "The fire didn't get so hot it completely burned him up. He was sitting with his butt in a damp place, and the seat of his britches and his wallet didn't get burned."

"I hope he passed out before the flames got him," Grace murmured. "He was our mailman all the time I was growing up. Nice old guy. Just couldn't leave the bottle alone."

"Chase don't think he's got no family around," Frankie offered. "Don't know who we should notify about this."

"Call Matt Frazee over at First Christian," I suggested. "He does funerals for people who don't have anyone. When the paper runs the story, I think a few of the people on Tug's old mail route will show up. Matt will give him a good send-off."

Frankie headed for the door. "And could you cover things for the next few hours?" I asked. "Marti still has a couple of items on her list I didn't get to."

"You got it, Boss," Frankie said. I dropped the curtain on the window as he headed back to the reception desk.

"I don't want to make light of another's death," Rosario said with a chuckle, "but an old guy burning himself up in a tree he'd stopped to sleep in? In all my years with the Bureau, that's the strangest thing I've come across."

"Maybe not," I said, turning to Grace. "How was your morning?"

"How long has it been since you were up on Webber's Mountain, Tate?" she asked as an opener.

I shrugged. "I haven't been up there since I came back to Crayton. It's probably been twenty years."

Grace grinned. "Well, the old house probably looks pretty much the same on the outside. But they've painted the inside. That main room where they do their readings? It's sort of a pale yellow. But they painted all around the furniture that was against the walls. Everything behind it is still plain wood. And they're both so much older than I remember them. I still can't tell one from the other, but they're looking real old."

I turned to Rosario whose smile was now one of amused curiosity.

"These old twin sisters have lived on a hilltop down in the corner of the county since they were born," I explained. "I think maybe their grandpappy built the place out of lumber he milled himself. They practically never come into town. When they do, they call Chase Backman who runs the ambulance service. He drives down there, brings them into town for whatever they need, then hauls them back."

Grace jumped back in, anxious that our Washington visitor not think the sisters to be just a couple of loonies. "But they're the nicest old women you could ask to meet. They have to heat their water in an old enamel stove and wash in a big metal tub, but they're always clean and well kept. And aside from the paint job, their house is real tidy. They do readings for people in the county. Tea leaves."

Rosario nodded skeptically.

"What did they have to say about their reading for Lilia Haddad?" I asked.

"She's been there three or four times."

"The reading she mentioned when we visited the house."

"No more than Raca told us. They said they both saw death in the leaves. That it was someone Lilia knew, and it was nearby."

Rosario cocked his head to the side. "They saw this in tea leaves?"

Grace shrugged. "That's what the Haddad women told us. Before this all happened, she'd been up to see the Webbers about how her family in Syria was doing. They told her they saw death. Someone she knew and that it was close. The sisters confirmed it. I don't pretend to understand it, but that's what both said."

I grinned over at Grace. "Did you have them do a reading for you?"

Her face reddened and she looked past me at nothing in particular. "I didn't have to ask. They insisted. I don't think they get a lot of company."

"And . . . ?"

The flush deepened. "Nothing we need to talk about here."

Rosario relaxed back into his chair. "So these two old ladies said they saw death coming. They obviously didn't have anything to do with it and didn't help prevent it in any way. If they can't tell you who did it, I'm not sure what that does for us."

Grace looked around hesitantly. "That wasn't all I learned. And maybe this can help in some way."

We all turned to her, waiting.

"Mrs. Haddad had been back. She went again the day after we left their house. The twins said she asked if they could tell her if others would come."

"And what did they have to say this time?" Rosario smiled skeptically.

Grace furrowed her brow and glanced at me sideways, as if this was something she would just as soon not have to say. "They told her they saw more death. And this time, they said her husband would be involved. And that great sadness would come to her from someone in her family."

Since neither Joseph nor our new agent had spoken to the Syrians, they decided to spend the afternoon questioning the Haddads. Marti called out to Kilgore Homes to talk to the plant manager, Roy Moser, about letting the Haddad men off for a few hours to meet with the investigators. She'd known Roy since they were kids, and Marti has a way of making even the most burdensome request seem like she's doing you a favor. She got Roy to send the brothers home by telling him someone had come all the way from Washington to talk to them, and the plant might get some positive national TV coverage if "this immigrant relocation story pans out." I got ahold of Yusef on his cell, told him to expect an FBI agent at his apartment, and to keep his brothers and their families nearby. Grace reluctantly agreed to go with me to talk to Verl and LJ Greaves. We headed out to Blackjack Holler.

"Blackjack" makes it sound like the holler ought to be some gamblers' hangout. But it's named after a tough, gnarly variety of oak that grows along the creekbanks with bark that looks like an armor of small, black, rectangular plates. Most folk think the wood isn't much good for anything but fence posts and fuel for the barbecue grill. The holler is a fitting location for the sovereign nation of two tough, gnarly old geezers who people around the county view as about as useful.

I mentioned before that Mara Joseph had once shot LJ Greaves. He and his son Verl are survivalist types who call eighty acres and a corrugated metal building in the bottomland along Mill Creek their sovereign homeland. When Joseph and I had gone down there nearly a year ago to talk to them about the death of their neighbor, Verl greeted us by shattering a persimmon tree beside the patrol car with a rifle shot as we crawled down their rutted excuse for a drive. Joseph had bailed from the cruiser and disappeared, showing up ten minutes later behind the two men while they were threatening to remove my manhood with one of their firearms if I didn't get off their property.

LJ's been known to let his meanness get the better of his judgment, and he made the mistake of swinging his 12-gauge around in Joseph's direction. Before he could level the thing, she dropped him with a shot to the right side. As it turned out, the men had nothing to do with the neighbor's death but had been poaching her timber and saw that as just as much reason to keep people away from their place. The encounter convinced me it was best to take Grace along on this visit.

A small box with a hooded lens hung from a post at the top of the quarter-mile drive that descended into the holler. Below it, a sign declared "No Trespassing – and that means YOU!" The Greaves would know we were coming. I stopped the Explorer halfway down the hill where a line of cedars still screened us from the house and climbed out.

"Verl, it's Sheriff Tate," I shouted through the trees. "I need to talk to you and LJ."

The snarl of the Greaves' pit bulls answered me, followed by a "Shut the hell up!" that immediately silenced the dogs. They'd been victims of the Greaves' wrath often enough to know when to obey.

"You know you ain't welcome down here, Tate," Verl called back.

"I just need to talk to you and LJ. I'm not here to cause you any trouble."

"You don't come out here lest there's trouble. And we got nothing to talk to you about. This is sovereign land, and you're trespassing."

"Like I told you last time I came, Verl, I can come back with a small army of state police or come down and talk to you peaceably. I have Officer Torres with me."

He was silent for a moment, then yelled, "You mean the looker? Not that little bitch what shot LJ?"

I looked over at Grace who still sat in the passenger seat, rolling her eyes.

"Yeah. Just the two of us. We'll leave our weapons in the car and walk down if that will make you feel better." Grace turned toward me with a start, silently mouthing "*No way!*"

"Or maybe it will just be me," I called. "Do you want me to come down now, or return with a lot of backup?"

Another moment of silence. Not even the dogs whimpered.

"Okay. You come on down," Verl hollered up at us. "And you can bring that Mexican woman. But leave your guns in the car."

I unbuckled my weapon and tossed it onto the seat, signaling for Grace to stay put. She cast me a disgusted glare and climbed from the far side of the Explorer, tucking her own weapon beneath the seat. We walked together around the cedars and into view of the metal building. Verl stood beside a rusting engine hoist that served as a yard ornament for the front of the Greaves' homestead.

What the pair called home was a 30' by 70' metal box with a wide pull-down garage door in the front beside a smaller walk-in entrance. A grimy window in the side door was covered on the inside by a faded yellow curtain. Aside from an open patch in front that held the engine hoist, a half-dozen fifty-gallon drums, and the dog pen, the ground around the building was a salvage yard of broken-down pickups, rusted riding mowers, and assorted axles, drivetrains, and rimless tires. In a cleared area in the rear, an aging GMC pickup with a heavy welded grate and front-mounted winch sat beside a small dozer and a stack of oak and walnut logs.

Verl leaned against the hoist with the same Marlin 336 that had threatened me last time in his right hand, resting it across the crook in his left elbow. He's a bull of a man, head shaved smooth as a cue ball and lower face covered by a thick tangle of rusty beard. A roll of belly fat hung over the waist of his stained jeans, spreading the buttons of a plaid, long-sleeved shirt.

"I see you been getting your trees cut," I called down to him as we approached.

He glanced back at the stack of logs. "Most of ours is down. That lady who took over Nettie's place after she died has been letting us cut hers for shares. I hope you ain't here about that."

"Got nothing to do with that, Verl. But I'm glad to see you're getting what you can cut before you have to move out."

"We ain't movin'," he growled. "Suing the bastards for invading our territory."

We stopped thirty feet from the man. He gave Grace an appreciative stare. She returned the look with an unwavering glare.

"How's that going?" I asked about the suit.

"Ain't heard nothin' back. But we ain't movin'. Pa's too sick to even be getting out of his chair. He ain't ever recovered from bein' shot by that other woman you brought down here."

I lifted my arms away from my hips. "No guns this time, Verl. Are you getting some medical help for LJ? Doc Waterman would come out and have a look at him."

"I'm gettin' him what he needs. What do you want?"

Grace decided she wanted to be more than just window dressing. "You must have heard the explosion a few days ago from here. What do you know about it?"

Verl sneered. "I know what it was. Someone must have wanted the dam gone as bad as we do."

"Did you hear what caused the explosion?" Grace asked.

"Just that it wasn't no accident. Someone did it."

"How did they do it?"

"Beats the hell out of me. It sounded pretty damn big. Dynamite, I'd guess."

"Do you have any dynamite in the house, Verl?"

The sneer returned to what we could see of his face behind the ragged beard. "So—we finally get to what you're here for. You're comin' after us again, are you, Tate? Time for you to be headin' on back up the hill."

I rescued the conversation from Grace. "It's just like with Nettie's death, Verl. We're checking with everyone close who might know something."

"And asking them if they have dynamite? I 'spect you'll be wantin' to come in and have a look around." He let the Marlin drop from the crook in his arm, aiming it at the ground midway between us.

"That would help you, Verl. If we don't see anything that could be used to blow up a dam, it might mean we don't need to bring some extra troops in to search your place."

Verl's face curled into a thoughtful frown. "You did right by me last time, Tate," he said finally. "Didn't screw me over when everyone thought we'd killed Nettie and taken a shot at that trooper bitch. I guess you can walk on through and see we don't got nothin'. But Pa's in bad shape, so don't be botherin' him. And don't be messing with things." He turned and led us toward the smaller door.

"Better take a deep breath," I whispered to Grace. "And watch where you step."

The inside of the Greaves' building made the outside look like the Webber sisters' tearoom and was even more chaotic than I remembered. Food-crusted dishes, discarded food packaging, and empty beer cans lay ankle-deep across a kitchen area to the right as we entered. The sharp stench of rancid meat mixed with the stale mustiness of mold and mildew clouded the air like swamp gas. I sneaked a glance at Grace whose nose had curled involuntarily. She was swallowing hard to keep her gag reflex from triggering.

A propane stove vented to the outside through the metal sidewall and a length of insulated PVC pipe brought cold water into a single tap from a well somewhere outside the building. The plastic sink below it overflowed with grimy pans, one a quarter-inch thick with bacon grease.

The front space opposite the kitchen was a jumble of sofas and chairs, some pushed into the background and stacked on top of each other as they split a seam or cracked across a vinyl cushion. The more serviceable seats formed a crude circle, grouped around an assortment of coffee and end tables, each heaped with worn tools, machine parts, grease-covered clothing, and more discarded food wrappers. LJ Greaves reclined in a worn, Naugahyde rocker, as pale as death in the dim light of the bare bulbs that hung from open trusses. His eyes were loosely closed, his mouth gaping open to draw long, rattling breaths.

I turned to Verl. "You need to get someone here to check LJ," I insisted. "He looks real bad."

Verl shook his head. "I can help him with what he needs. I ain't havin' no one comin' in here to be poking around. You get on with what you need to do."

"If I send the Doc out, will you let him take a look at him?"

"You send him out and I'll shoot him," Verl said without the slightest hint of exaggeration.

A channel no wider than the men's shoulders disappeared into the back of the building between the nearest sofa and the mounds of kitchen rubble, cast in the dim light of the open front door. Both sides were stacked head-high with furniture that had moved beyond the slightly-damaged stage and was now useless. Crates of car, tractor, and mower parts, old TVs, bicycles, vacuums, and worn tires bumped against the metal trusses overhead. We picked our way systematically through the kitchen clutter and around the snoring LJ, looking for anything that might resemble an explosive pack. Grace unclipped a flashlight from her belt and started toward the shadowy passage.

"Hang on a minute," I called, turning to Verl. "You got any of those boobytraps set up, Verl? I don't want Officer Torres to be tripping one of your shotguns."

He sneered over at me. "Ain't put them up again since you sent them state troopers through here last time. They said they was lettin' us off since nobody'd been killed. But would be haulin' us in if they ever found them set up again. A man can't even protect his own property in this police state."

"Not with boobytraps," I said, flashing my own light at the floor in the channel. No wires that I could see. "Keep an eye open for trips as you go through there," I cautioned Grace, and followed her into the slot canyon of junk.

The rear of the building was split into halves like the front. Two unmade double beds filled the back left corner, the hoard piles stacked right up to the side of one, the second pressed tight against the outer wall. There was just enough room to squeeze between them, with a goose-necked lamp separating the headboards.

The corner to the right was the only spot in the building that allowed any free movement. Four chairs surrounded an oval table. A long workbench hugged an outside wall with a flatscreen TV at one end, the rest covered with cartridge reloading equipment. Between the bench and a rear door, an open cabinet held an assortment of weapons: two standard hunting rifles, four shotguns, two semi-automatic rifles that looked like AR-15s, and a shelf of assorted handguns and ammunition. Grace went directly to the cabinet while I picked through the junk that covered the table. Verl stood in the gap between walls of scrap, the Marlin still hanging from one hand.

"You men have a computer?" I asked.

He scoffed. "What the hell for? We got no need and wouldn't know what to do with it if we had one. Them things ruinin' the world anyway. People spread all kinds of socialist shit through that social media."

"You've got a TV."

"Like to watch them shows about people living in Alaska. Thinkin' of doin' that when LJ gets fit."

"You got a satellite antenna?"

"Up on top."

"Is that TV a smart screen?"

"What the hell does that mean? A smart screen? It's just a plain old TV."

"How about your phones? You still got your cell phones?"

"Yeah. I got a phone. LJ quit payin' on his. He's been too stoved up to use it. You gotta go up to the road to get a good signal."

"How about letting Officer Torres take yours up to the road to have a look at it?

"What the hell for?"

"To see if you used it to order anything in the last couple of months."

"With my phone? You mean like callin' for some dynamite?"

"Yes. Something like that. It will save us having to go get the judge to give us permission to take it. In fact, I'd probably need to take it with me anyway to keep you from getting rid of the thing."

Verl's free hand involuntarily went to his pocket. He frowned deeply for a silent moment, then pulled out what looked like an iPhone 5 in a cracked plastic case. "Don't make no difference to me. I hardly use the thing."

I took it and handed it to Grace. "Send a list of calls for the past two months to Marti and check the search history back as far as it shows," I told her. "See if anything catches your eye. You got a password, Verl?"

"Yeah. Just them first four numbers."

Grace exited through the rear door. As I moved on to a stack of army green ammunition boxes, the Explorer rumbled to life and climbed out of the holler. She returned fifteen minutes later. I was just confirming that the last of the metal cases had nothing in it. She came through the same rear door, dropped Verl's phone in a clear space on the table, and looked around for other things to examine with no indication she felt an urgent need to talk to me.

"I think we've seen about what we need to, Verl," I said. "We're just getting into this investigation, so may need to come back. But we're through for now. Thanks for being cooperative."

"Ain't really cooperation when I'm just keepin' you from

bringin' the storm troopers in," he grumbled.

"Well, thanks anyway. And get LJ in to see a doctor. He doesn't look good."

"I can take care of Pa," he repeated and stayed planted in the narrow passage while we left through the back.

"I take it there wasn't anything too interesting on the phone," I guessed as we skirted the building. Grace nodded without looking over.

"I sent a list of calls to Marti. There weren't many. Not even one a day. And there was nothing in his browser history. I checked to make sure it hadn't been purged. I don't think he even knows how to use the data functions. There's no signal at all down here, so I doubt he experiments with it much."

I sniffed. "Wouldn't surprise me. And what a pit that place is! But I didn't see any reason to start picking through all those piles of crap. It's like one of those games where you stack up the blocks. You pull out the wrong piece and the whole place collapses on you."

"Jenga," she said.

"What?"

"That's the game. Jenga."

We had reached the car and looked back to find Verl standing in the open front doorway, Marlin still in hand.

"You don't seem to think the Greaves blew up the dam," Grace ventured as we climbed in. "Otherwise you'd have wanted to risk an avalanche."

I started the engine and swung the cruiser around between the rusting yard ornaments. "Your phone check convinced me. LJ looks like he's on the verge of death. Verl wouldn't be bringing anyone in to stay with him, and it seems pretty obvious he won't leave him alone. With no computer, no indication of web activity on the phone, and no trips away from the holler, how would they get an M183 pack?"

"Someone brought it to them?"

"They'd still have to ask. Let's see who the calls were to. If they have some survivalist buddies they call, we may have new reason to worry. But right now, I believe we need to be looking somewhere else for our bomber."

"For whoever killed the man?"

I shook my head uncertainly. "I'm still thinking that if the killer wanted him found, why bury him? And even if he did decide to dig him back up, there were sure a hell of a lot easier ways."

Grace tipped her head in reluctant agreement. "So, what do we do now?"

Instead of turning back toward town, I steered left toward the highway north. "I think we go see who was checked in at the Hampton at the same time as our Mr. Sayegh."

11

Grace tapped and swiped at her phone as we drove toward Springfield. "There are three or four hotels within a stone's throw of the Hampton on 65," she observed. "We may need to check them all."

"We will," I agreed. "But if you were following this guy to find the right time to get rid of him, where would you be?"

Grace nodded. "Yes. I'd want to be where I could stay right with him if he left. That pretty well means being in the same place."

"Either that or staying out of sight in the parking lot. If Sayegh knew the man who was after him, that may have been the case. But I'm betting he didn't. So probably the same hotel."

Grace tilted her head thoughtfully. "There's two assumptions in that statement I'm not sure we can make." I turned away and smiled at my reflection in the window. I was about to get a dose of that police training she had and I didn't. Rule One: never assume anything. Even little things. One wrong assumption and you're headed off in completely the wrong direction. I'd learned to listen to her, act like I'd been considering what she said all along, and adjust as needed.

"First," she lifted a slender finger. "We can't assume Sayegh didn't know the person." Another finger. "And two, we don't know that person was a 'he.' The Haddads knew him. And he knew them and where they were. I can see this being like a Syrian mafia hit where both sides have their hitmen. In this case, the Haddad side got to Sayegh before he got to them."

"But Rosario said there had been other interceptions," I reminded her. "Not all Syrian. And each with the *nazars* left somewhere on the body." I wanted to convince her there was a pretty good basis for my assumptions before I conceded. "This must be a bigger operation than just a Syrian family feud. But you're right. We shouldn't assume a 'he.' My bad. And we'll check out the nearby places just to be safe."

I'd called Joseph as we left town and asked her to contact a Springfield judge she'd once dated to see if he could sign warrants that would allow us to review hotel registration records for the previous month. She called when we were still thirty minutes from the city.

"Stop by the Greene County Courthouse and he'll have them for you. You just need to let him know what hotels you want to search."

"It looks like there will be four," I told her.

"Shouldn't be a problem. His clerk will have them waiting."

We started with the Hampton, getting a printout of data on everyone who had registered up to a week before Farid Sayegh checked in and left during the two days following his death. The Syrian had been at the hotel for four days, which limited the pool considerably. Only seven guests had been registered during that full period, and in only four rooms. The same proved to be the case at the other three hotels that were close enough we thought they might be reasonable possibilities. We ended up with a list of twenty-seven guests and fourteen rooms.

As we drove back toward Crayton, the sun had dropped below the horizon, turning the wisps of horsetail clouds that brushed the sky a filmy violet. Grace flipped on the overhead light and scanned our lists.

"Let's say this guy was watching our man so he could follow him wherever he went. The Hampton has doors on all four sides. If he hadn't bugged Sayegh's room somehow, how would he keep track of him without there being at least two people? Maybe even more, since he'd need to be watching day and night?"

Another question that reminded me that even after nearly a year and a half, I'm still a rookie at this job. I thought about it for a good two minutes before answering. She didn't push.

"First of all," I said finally, "I noticed you said 'he.' We have a number of women on our list, so they aren't out yet."

She gave me a begrudging elbow in the shoulder. "Okay, smartass. He or she."

"But you raise a good point. We can't just look at singles. But we can't eliminate them either. I can see a professional getting into Sayegh's room and planting a camera, or even just a buzzer of some kind on the door. It would let him—or *her*—know when the man came and went. If they knew where his car was parked, when they saw him leave the room they could get to their own vehicle in time to follow."

"That pretty well brings us back to the killer staying at the Hampton."

"Or," I added, having one of those stomach-sinking moments, "he was living in his car in the Hampton lot, like we said before. We should have asked to get copies of their parking surveillance tapes for the past three weeks."

She chuckled. "We're back to 'he' again, I see."

"Okay. Let's forget the pronouns for now and just worry about how he did it."

Grace arched a thoughtful brow. "There's only one drive out of the Hampton lot, so one person could keep an eye on it. Watching from a car seems like it might be a pretty good possibility, now that I think about it."

"I like the door buzzer idea better. One person could handle it then. He could sleep in his clothes and be ready to move. I wonder if the Patrol looked at the room Sayegh stayed in? The killer might have left the device in place."

"I'm going with the car in the lot," Grace insisted. "If they haven't already, get Officer Joseph to ask one of her guys to check the room for a bug of some type and call about a warrant for the security tapes." She waved the printouts in front of me. "While you and Marti start through these lists, I'll drive back up in the morning and get the videos."

12

Initial review of the lists, it turned out, had to wait. Following the Springfield trip with Grace, I'd again come in early and found Marti already at her desk. Plopping the sheets in front of her, I went to the coffeemaker and poured us both a cup.

"Want a bit of a break today?" I asked as she flipped through the pages. "Grace is making a run back to Springfield to pick up some video. We need to contact these people, see why they were in Springfield at the same time our victim was there, and follow up on alibis."

Marti deposited the sheets back on her desktop. "Grace called just before you came in. She's got some other things she has to take care of today. And Officer Joseph needed a little more time to get warrants. Plus . . ." she said, smiling slyly, ". . . you forgot about job shadowing this morning, didn't you?"

"*Damn*," I said, before adding "Pardon my French. But was that today? I forgot all about it. Who do I have?"

"Miriam Haddad. The school said she asked for you specifically."

"Miriam's interested in law enforcement?" The girl was Yusef's youngest daughter, a sophomore, and one I'd been helping with parent-teacher conferences when only Lilia could attend.

"Maybe it's you she's interested in," Marti suggested with a teasing grin.

"The kid's only fifteen."

"Yup. That's about the right age."

"I can't imagine the school sending her out on patrol with me alone. Not with all the concerns they have about safety nowadays."

Marti chuckled. "Are you a threat, Sheriff?"

"You know what I mean. They'd want her going with Grace."

"She asked for you."

"Then, they'd want someone riding along."

"They do—and asked if we had anyone. I told them we did."

"Yeah? Who?"

Her grin widened. "Me. You get me."

"Double damn!" I said without apology. "Not that I don't want you going along. But I'd like to get started on these lists."

She turned back to the printouts. "Maybe Rocky can spend his morning in here helping with them."

I pulled the top sheet off the stack. "Yeah. I can't very well sit in the office all morning and call hotel guests while Miriam twiddles her thumbs. Not the way to maintain the fascinating lawman image."

Marti handed me another list from her desk. "There are two or three other things that need attention. A couple there I'd rather not assign to Frankie."

At the top of the sheet, boldly underlined, was the name <u>Farley Buzzard</u>. "What does old Farley need?" I asked.

"Something's been killing his goats."

I chuckled. "We'll take Miriam out there. If she *is* thinking about law enforcement, that should cure the kid. I know he butchers goats for the Haddads. She might as well see where some of her meals are coming from."

"She may never want to eat again," Marti snorted. "That's a pretty rough way to start a job shadowing day. I drove out there with Nolan to deliver a load of feed corn once. Farley was walking us out to his feed shed when he stopped halfway and said he needed to take a leak. Then he said, 'Don't be shocked if this comes out orange. It's the meds I'm taking.' So he stopped right there and did the job."

"Was it orange?"

"Well, I'm sure, Tate! I wasn't about to stand there and watch the man relieve himself. . . . But yes. Nolan said it was orange."

I chuckled. "I'll bet no one will have better stories when they report back to class tomorrow."

"Yes," Marti muttered. "If they're stories the girl can share in school."

Miriam showed up promptly at 8:30. She's a gangly teen, a few inches taller than her sister Raca, but with the same wide mouth, dark eyes, and heavy brows. She's still struggling to catch up with her adolescent growth spurt and is inclined to wrap herself in a hug that hides her blossoming chest. Marti asked if she'd like a Coke or bottle of water to take along. She already had one in her backpack. Marti grabbed a jacket and was dialing Rocky's cell before we were through the door.

I pointed the Explorer northwest out of town with Miriam examining buttons and switches on the dash and the Sig strapped to my hip. Marti sat quietly in the back, leaving the shadow in my hands.

"Have you ever had to use that thing?" Miriam asked, her eyes on the weapon.

"Once in a while. I rarely have to pull it. Just lay my hand on it to convince people I mean business."

"Have you ever shot anyone?"

"Not here. Hope I never have to."

"When you were in Iraq?"

Hmm. I'd really hoped to keep this conversation domestic. "Yes," I answered. "But not something I like to remember."

She became silent, fidgeting with her hands in her lap and looking out at passing farmland and stands of hardwoods as we left town.

I waited for Marti to fill the awkward silence. When she didn't, I said, "We're on our way to meet with a guy who can be a little different. I need to warn you about him before we get there." Her quick glance showed enough alarm that I immediately clarified.

"Oh, he's not dangerous. His name's Farley Buzzard and he raises meat goats on his farm up near Willston. In fact, I think your family buys meat from him."

"Buzzard? What kind of name is that?"

"I think his father was Cherokee. At least, that's the story." I waited for Marti to confirm. More silence.

"What's different about him?"

"Well, he's something of a hermit and has a tendency to say whatever pops into his head, without thinking about others being around. People sometimes get offended by things he says or does. So just ignore him if something comes out that shocks you."

"Like what?" she wanted to know.

"That's the problem," I admitted. "You never know what it's going to be with Farley. Maybe some cussing. Maybe some crude comment—or him doing something odd."

"I'm not shocked very easily," she insisted.

I chuckled. "Neither am I, but sometimes he catches me off guard." I glanced at Marti in the mirror. She was just smiling silently.

"Is he married?" Miriam asked.

"No. Never has been. That's probably one of the problems. There's no one to tell him he needs to be more careful about what he says and does."

"Why are we going up there?

"Something's been killing his goats. He called to see if we could come out and give him some help."

"What do you think's been doing it?" Her eyes again showed worry.

"I have an idea. But I want to see what he has to say before I make a judgment." We turned off the gravel county road onto an unkept lane that wandered back through a thick stand of cedars to the front of a trailer that could have doubled for Tug Divine's. It stood without skirting on six square stacks of concrete blocks. Heavy woven cables strapped it to steel rings that protruded from the ground at each end, keeping the thing from blowing off its crude foundation. A set of rough wooden steps rose to a central door that opened as we pulled up in front. The man who stepped onto the shallow porch caused Miriam to shrink back into her seat.

To say Farley Buzzard is grizzly does a disservice to the bears. He's massive enough to qualify, but no self-respecting bear would allow himself to become so unkempt. The man's leathered face peered out between a mop of grey-brown hair and beard. Both looked as if he'd grabbed the wire on an electric fence and hung on for dear life. He wore a stained red T-shirt under bib overalls that had never seen a good wash. He frowned disapprovingly, hands thrust deep into his pockets.

"Who you got there with ya, Tate?" he called before we could leave the Explorer.

Marti and I stepped out of the cruiser. Miriam stayed pressed into the passenger seat.

"You know Marti Bleasdale. And we have a student from the high school with us. They have the kids go out and work with someone for a day to see what the job's like. This is Miriam Haddah. Her father, Yusef, buys goats from you."

"Well, sure thing! Them Moslem families. Come on out here, girl, and let me have a look at you," he bellowed. Miriam cautiously stepped out beside the vehicle, letting the door shield her from the burly man.

"Come on around here. I can't see who you are when you're hidin' back there." She eased around the front of the Explorer and stood beside me.

"Hmm," he grunted. "Looks like you could use a little more of my meat on your bones." While she tightened the hug across her chest, he nodded his willingness to let her join us. "Come on around back. I'll show you what I was callin' about." He marched down the steps, hands still in his pockets, and led us around the end of the trailer. A twenty-foot loafing shed stood at one end of a bare patch of earth that was surrounded by hog panels wired to rusty orange T-posts to form a corral. Thirty boar goats, white-bodied with brown heads and long drooping ears, huddled together in the enclosure, a dozen miniature kids hiding among their protecting legs. The animals were taller than most of their breed, with the round, full bodies of sheep and strong, straight legs. The rams that looked at us warily from each end of the herd had rough, coffee-colored horns that swept down and back along their necks. It was hard to imagine another animal bringing one down. Farley leaned against one of the posts.

"I got 'em all penned up 'til I can figure out what's killing 'em," Farley growled, then released a blast of methane from the seat of his overalls that echoed off the side of the trailer behind us. He lifted his nose to the wind and said, as if commenting on the weather, "Hey! I think I heard a buck snort."

I glanced over at Marti who had turned to hide her face. Miriam stared at the seat of the big man's coveralls, dumbfounded.

Farley pushed away from the fence. "But come here an' look at this," he said, leading us along the wall of panels.

At the end of the pen away from the loafing shed, a battered red Chevy pickup stood beside the makeshift corral, its tailgate down and a white, curly mass stretched across the bed. As we got closer, I could see that it was Farley's Pyrenees, Rupert. The dog's neck was splashed dark purple across the back.

"Whatever it was got Rupert first." The big man's voice cracked and he cleared his throat gruffly. "Didn't mess with the dog, once he killed him. Just left him there for dead. But then got one of my does. I left her out in the pasture cause her guts was all tore out and half of her was eaten away. Thought it might keep the thing from comin' up closer to the house." Miriam had been trailing close behind and shrunk back a step.

I laid a hand on the stiff, still body of the dog. "Damn shame," I said, starting with what I knew was most important to the ragged old herder. "Rupert was a good 'un."

"I'm so sorry," Marti said quietly, and we both waited long enough for the man to know we meant it. Then I asked, "What's your thinking on this, Farley? You got any ideas?"

"I know what it looks like. But so far, we ain't seen any 'round here."

I parted the hair on the dog's neck and inspected the bite. "Pretty clean. No tearing. And the canines look two to three inches apart. Gotta have powerful jaws to do this. I'd say cougar instead of coyote."

"No coyote could get Rupert," Farley insisted. "He's killed 'em before. Two or three in a night when they come at him in a pack. This thing ambushed him. Like from a tree."

"We've had a couple of sightings down in the south part of the county," I told him. "And one got hit up on I-44 west of Springfield. They're around."

"What can I do to stop them?" He stroked the head of the dead animal with a rough hand. "I gotta find a new dog. Gonna be hard to find one as good as Rupert."

I nodded. "He was a good one," I said again. "You want some help burying him somewhere?"

Farley shook his head. "I'll do it myself. Need to spend a little more time with the old boy. But what about this lion?"

"I'll call Conservation. Have Jess Traynor come out. They'll want to know about it and can help you trap the thing or hunt it down. If it's killing livestock, they'll want to get rid of it." I thought for a moment, then asked, "You didn't hear Rupert making a fuss? Pyrenees usually make a racket as soon as anything comes near."

Farley shrugged his massive shoulders. "Like I say, I think he got ambushed. Sprung on him from above or something." He frowned down at the guard dog. "But I h'aint been payin' the attention I normally do. My innards has all been balled up, Tate. H'aint had a good shit in over a week."

I glanced again at Miriam whose eyes had doubled in size and jaw dropped open. Marti was out of sight behind us. I tried to look thoughtful.

"Might be good to be checked. That can get to be serious if you let it go."

Farley's mouth disappeared into his chin fur. "Naw. I got her taken care of. Got a piece of coat hanger and pried out the turd that was blockin' me up."

I had to turn away, clamping my own jaw shut to stifle a belly laugh. When sure I could keep it under control, I muttered, "You need to be careful about that, too, Farley. You'll be injuring yourself inside."

"Hell, I know that," he mumbled. "I bent a loop in the thing so's it didn't have no points. Slid in there pretty easy. Think I got her cleared out."

I turned and winked at Miriam. "Glad you got the plumbing working," We started back toward the front of the trailer. "This is one I think Conservation will want to get involved in. I'll call them on the way back to town. You sure I can't help you with Rupert?"

"I got it," he said. "Thanks for coming out, Tate." He turned to Miriam. "You learn anything, girl?"

She pressed her mouth into a firm, tight line to suppress a smile and nodded quickly. "Sheriff Tate said it would be interesting," she said. "And I'm really sorry about your dog."

He nodded grimly. "He was a good 'un. But life goes on."

She turned with me and headed toward the car, the girl again clutching at her sides as if cramps were rippling through her thin body. Before we were completely turned in the drive, she began to sputter as if she'd gulped a mouthful of water into her lungs.

"You okay?" I asked, glancing over to see her nodding in short bobs while she struggled to contain her laughter.

"You learn anything, girl?" I asked in my best imitation of Farley's gravelly bass.

Mariam couldn't hold it in any longer, doubling forward against her seatbelt, her laughter growing with every bump in Farley's rutted lane. The sight of the girl struck us like the blast from the seat of the goat man's filthy overalls, and Marti and I began to chuckle with her. The craziness of the morning swept through the car like a case of the flu. When we reached the county road, I managed to steer the cruiser onto the shoulder. With the radio crackling a morning report about a heavy backup on US 60, we clutched red-faced at our sides and guffawed like drunken sailors, tears streaming down the girl's blush-tinted cheeks while Marti threw open her door to gasp for air.

When I was able to focus again on driving, I pulled out onto the county road and turned toward town. Miriam pulled a Kleenex from her pocket, wiped at her eyes, and took a couple of long, slow breaths. She glanced back quickly at Marti, who was still sniffling, then over at me. Seeing the two of us laugh ourselves silly seemed to have given the girl permission to tell me why she'd wanted this ride-along in the first place. She glanced shyly again at Marti, then said, "Mr. Tate, I've heard people say you were going to marry an Arab woman. Is that true?"

Ahh. Here it came! "Yes. That's true," I said, smiling over at her.

"Where was she from?"

"Chicago. But we met in Bahrain where we were both interpreters for the U.S. Embassy there."

"Where was her family from?" She glanced at me in quick bursts, diverting her eyes back to the passing fields.

"Her family was Palestinian. Her parents came to the states when they were forced out of their home in the Golan Heights back in the nineteen-sixties. A town called Quneitra."

"Oh, yeah. We went down there as a family once. To where we could look over into the Golan Heights. There were still some big Palestinian camps in Syria then, not too far from there." Her mind wandered off for a silent moment, then she asked, "She was Muslim?"

"Yes. Not especially devout, but she called herself Muslim."

"And her parents were alright with her marrying you?"

I couldn't stifle a chuckle. We were five minutes past Farley Buzzard's bent coat hanger and Miriam Haddad was deep into my personal life. What was this all about?

"No," I admitted. "I'd say they weren't alright with it. But I didn't have any problem with her being whatever she wanted to be, so they were beginning to come around."

"And then she died?" She finally looked over and kept her eyes on me, wondering, I think, what emotion might show. I had told the story a hundred times, or a thousand, but never to a fifteen-year-old who seemed more than just curiously interested. I found myself doing my own window gazing to make sure she didn't see the quick blinking. Marti sat so still and quiet in the back, I knew she was trying to disappear. I nodded slowly, adding a few seconds to steady my voice.

"Yes. She was killed in a bomb attack in Baghdad where we'd been sent to do some interpreting."

"Baghdad? I thought you said Bahrain?"

"They shuffled us around sometimes when there were big events that needed interpreters. There were two things going on in Iraq that needed more people than they had in-country."

"Were you with her? When the attack happened?"

Blinking now didn't do the job. I felt a tear escape down the side of my nose and knew she saw it.

"I'm sorry," she said quietly. "It's none of my business."

I sniffed the tear away and gave her a lame smile. "No. I don't mind talking about it. But it's not the finest moment in my life, and it's still a little hard for me to think about. I wasn't with her. It was my job to decide who on our team went to which location. I sent her to a hotel in the city where there was some kind of visiting group that needed guides. I took an embassy party. Worst decision of my life."

She looked over with a serious frown and asked softly, "How did you decide?" I'd rationalized this over and over and wasn't sure what was true anymore, but I told her the version I'd finally worked out. "The group at the hotel was there on some WHO mission. World Health Organization. Most were women. I thought they'd appreciate having a woman interpreter. Plus, Adeena spoke fluent French, and there was a French delegation. At the embassy party, there were some US senators that I thought maybe I could make some points with. Pretty selfish on my part."

"It wasn't your fault," she murmured in the same muted tones. "You couldn't have known. And the women thing makes sense to me."

"I did know that I was inside the Green Zone, and she was outside," I admitted, wondering why I was sharing all this with a job shadowing ride-along fifteen-year-old kid. "Just by location, she wasn't as safe."

Her head shook rapidly back and forth. "I was thirteen when we left Syria. I remember the war. You could never know where you were going to be safe. The Embassy could have been the target as easily as the hotel. You just couldn't know."

Maybe that was it. I knew the girl was less than two years away from living in the middle of rocket and gas attacks. "Yes," I said. "Your family would understand better than anyone here. And thank you for helping me feel a little better about it."

"It was a terrible place to be," she muttered to herself, wrapping her arms again to squeeze away a shudder.

We rode without speaking, neither wanting to think again of war and loss. I checked Marti in the mirror. Her eyes blinked quietly back at me. Miriam finally broke the silence. "Did you worry about marrying someone from such a different background?"

Someone, I thought, is showing some interest in this pretty girl, and she's not certain how to deal with it.

"We had the advantage of her growing up in the states, just as I did," I said. "But there was still the Chicago versus the Missouri Ozarks thing. And Muslim versus . . .well, not much of anything. We did worry about that a little."

"Yeah. That would be something. How did *your* parents feel about it?"

"My father died when I was ten," I told her. "And my mother while I was in the service. By the time I met Adeena, there were no parents around to worry about it." I glanced over at her and chuckled. "My dad would have been really upset. He was a hardnosed old mill worker who'd spent a year in Vietnam when he was just a kid. Never talked about it much. But anything foreign was suspicious."

"Mmm," she murmured. "I know what that's like."

"My mother? She would have loved Adeena."

"Adeena? That's a pretty name," Miriam said. "I'll bet she was pretty."

"Very pretty," I agreed. This time, her eyes misted as only the eyes can of an adolescent girl who intensely feels every pang of love and loss, even when they belong to someone else. I again had to turn to my side window.

"You're not Muslim. That shouldn't be a problem for you," I suggested finally, thinking she might want to tell me why she wanted to know all this.

"No. But we're Syrian. Most people think all Syrians are Muslim. And we're Eastern Christians. When it comes to friends, that makes about the same difference to my mother and father. Especially my father." I waited, but that was all she wanted to say.

13

I have a personal obsession that fits perfectly with being a sheriff but will probably end up killing me. When some problem is unresolved, it eats at me like a cancer.

Our morning with Miriam had ended with a complimentary lunch in the school cafeteria: pepperoni pizza, canned green beans, tossed salad, and my favorite—chocolate milk. We would have suffered awkwardly through the meal had Marti not known every person in the cafeteria and enough about each family to keep some level of conversation going. We shared a round table with two other ride-along teams: one who spent the morning at the branch bank; one at a dog breeding kennel that specializes in boxers. The girl and I couldn't look at each other without visions of Farley stooped over with his coat hanger tickling a laugh that had to be smothered with a mouthful of pizza. Marti filled in nicely around us. The fourth period bell finally came to the rescue.

Marti and I escaped back to the office where Rocky had done a yeoman's job of screening the lists and had a summary waiting. He hadn't been able to reach four of the names, and two he had spoken to didn't have explanations that seemed satisfying. We shared the story of our morning with Miriam and Farley. Rocky had a few Buzzard stories of his own and laughed until he had to slip into the bathroom to douse his face with cold water. At 4:30, I called Mara Joseph about dinner.

We met at LeeAnn's café at 6:00. The regulars remembered her from her time in town with the Suskey case and welcomed her like an old friend. Three or four remembered her name.

"You can't exactly have an intimate little dinner in this town, can you?" she said, half-jokingly. "Reminds me of the theme song from the old Cheers series on TV. '*Sometimes you want to go where everybody knows your name. . . .'* And sometimes you don't. I guess in Crayton, you don't have much choice, unless you want to sit in your car at Sonic."

"They're just interested," I defended. "Good people. All of them."

"Interested in you and me being here? In why I'm down here? In what this case is about?"

"Yup. All of that. But mainly, just interested."

We finished the Wednesday prime rib special and ordered crème brulee, the talk turning back to the case as we waited. I found myself fingering my wine glass, smiling across at her as if captivated by her pretty face and every word she said, and thinking about those damn lists. My attentive gaze must not have been convincing. She stopped in mid-sentence, leaned back in her chair, and said, "Have you heard anything I've said?"

"Sure," I lied. "You were just telling me what you and Rosario thought needed to be done next on the dam bombing."

"And that was . . . ?"

"Well, let's see. You were . . . ."

"Yes. That's what I thought. You have no idea. Where have you been the last five minutes?"

No sense trying to bluff my way out of this one. She was right. I had no idea what she'd just said. "You got me," I confessed. "I've been thinking the name of the person we're looking for must be on one of those lists from the hotels, and it's driving me nuts."

"They'll be there in the morning. Give yourself a bit of a break. And it's important that you know what's going on with the rest of the case. Rosario's heading back to Washington in the morning. We found other fragments of a demo pack out at the site. Those military kits have been through a re-purposing in the last couple of years—and just in a couple of places. They're not available on the open market anywhere. It shouldn't be possible for someone to get ahold of one. He needs to find out if some have turned up missing at one of the munitions depots. That's as likely as your lists to lead us somewhere."

I committed to listen more attentively. "And makes it even *less* likely the Greaves were involved in this somehow. That should make you feel better. What are you planning to do while Rosario's gone?"

She grinned over at me. "I called again about the warrants you wanted for cameras covering parking areas. Grace should be able to pick them up in the morning. I thought if you were up to a houseguest tonight, I might help you and Marti finish up those lists you can't get out of your head. A 'guest room' type houseguest," she added quickly.

My mind was suddenly off hotel registrations. "We didn't resist each other very well the last time you stayed over," I reminded her. "You sure you want to risk that again?"

"That was my fault. And I promised you I wouldn't let it happen again."

"Hmm," I muttered. "I was hoping you might be weakening."

She tilted her head apologetically. "Sorry, Tate. But not about that. I'm still trying to get reassigned back to St. Louis. If I get too involved again, it's going to mess that all up."

"Then maybe staying at my place isn't a good idea."

"I *love* your place. It's the most peaceful place I've ever been. And it saves me a trip back to Springfield or a night at the Super 8. I can deal with it if you can. Climb in bed and think about hotel lists."

"I'll still be hoping you'll slip in beside me at 3:00 a.m. Last time that pretty well ended thoughts of anything else."

"As I recall, I found that you were more than ready when I arrived," she grinned. "But this time, can I stay as a friend without benefits?"

The phone buzzing in my shirt pocket interrupted my saying that I wasn't about to promise anything. I recognized the number as the health clinic.

"Sheriff Tate," I answered officially.

"Tate, this is Doc Waterman. I think you may want to get over here as soon as you can."

I lifted the cell from my cheek and looked at the time. 6:45 p.m. The clinic kept a nurse practitioner on duty until 7:00 on weekdays, but Doc Waterman usually managed to get away around 5:00. This must be something the NP didn't feel comfortable treating by herself.

"I'm at LeeAnn's," I told him. "I'll be there in five minutes." I gave Joseph a disappointed frown. "Something's up at the clinic. It's only a couple of blocks away, so I'll walk over. See if you can cancel the desserts and you can either come along, or drive out to my place and settle in. I'll be there as soon as I get whatever this is taken care of."

She folded her napkin onto the table and signaled the waiter. "I'll come with you. I'd just as soon not be at your place without you, especially when you don't know how long you'll be. Plus, I never know what interesting little challenge I'm going to run into when I go somewhere with you."

We walked the short distance to the clinic, found the outer door locked, but Doc Waterman conferring with the nurse practitioner in the empty waiting area. He hurried to the door and ushered us in, giving Joseph a familiar nod. "I'm glad you're here, Officer. This is one of those cases I don't want Tate handling by himself."

He led us to the rear of the building and into one of the examination rooms. Grace Torres hunched forward at the end of a paper-draped examination table, her left arm wrapped in a fresh cast. She looked up as we entered, curling a badly split lip and a swollen cheek and eye into a painful frown.

"Doc, I told you I didn't need any help," she muttered thickly.

"I knew you weren't going to go to your parents', and someone's going to have to look after you for a few days, Grace," the doctor said emphatically. "Too much activity and you're going to have permanent damage."

Joseph stepped self-consciously into a corner beside the door while I pulled a folding chair over and sat in front of my chief deputy. I took her hand, but she winced and pulled it quickly away. The knuckles were scraped raw and covered with salve. I let my hands fall into my lap.

"Did Sal do this to you, Grace?"

Her jaw tightened and her eyes filled in the corners, but she remained mute.

"I believe so," Doc Waterman answered for her. "When she came in, she said she'd been in what she called 'a bit of a domestic disagreement.'"

I reached toward the cheekbone that was already turning a bloodstained purple. "Any damage to the bone?" I asked, mainly to the doctor.

He stepped up beside me and gently encouraged Grace onto her feet. "No. But this isn't the worst of it." He began to turn her, but she resisted, casting Mara Joseph a glare that told her she wasn't welcome in the room. Joseph didn't need encouragement.

"I'll just step out," she said, moving quickly to the door, "and will be in the waiting area if you need anything."

With the door closed behind the state investigator, Grace was still hesitant.

"Please, Grace," the doctor encouraged. "Tate needs to see this." She reluctantly turned with her back toward me. Waterman gingerly lifted her shirt. Her ribs, from hip to shoulder blade, were an angry mass of bruises, broken by darker stripes where some hard object had pounded her side."

"We completed x-rays before I called," the doctor said, pointing to two midnight blue welts. "She has two fractured ribs about here, and I'm worried about a bruised kidney lower down. She needs to be off her feet for a week, then get checked again before she does more than light work."

I nodded grimly. "Doc, could you give us a minute alone?"

He lowered the shirt and slipped out of the room.

"What happened?" I asked, turning Grace back to face me and

helping her ease onto the table.

"The Webber sisters warned me," she said cryptically.

I dropped back onto the folding chair. "What did they tell you?"

"That they saw pain and injury. That I was going to be hurt." She paused, then added, "We had an argument."

"You and Sal?"

She dropped her eyes to the floor.

"One hell of an argument," I muttered. "What about?"

She sat in silence for a long moment, her battered face a mask. "About you," she said finally.

"About me?"

"He knew I'd ridden up to Springfield with you and thought I was going back with you today. He got all bent out of shape about it. It's happened before—like when we went to Muskogee and Tulsa when Nettie was killed. He doesn't like me taking trips with you. And when we were gone that overnight, he got really angry. But I've been able to calm him down before. This time was different."

"When we went overnight, nothing happened. And we weren't gone overnight this time. You were home at regular shift time."

She nodded sourly. "Yeah. But I made the mistake of talking about what we'd done. About getting the lists and about needing to go back today for video. He said I couldn't go."

"And you said . . . ?"

"I said that was my job. That's what I do."

"And . . . ?"

"He said, 'Not anymore.' He said he's tired of his friends telling him they wouldn't let any woman of theirs run around with another man like I do. I told him I wasn't his woman, and I'd go wherever I damn well pleased with you. That's when he hit me in the face."

"Why did he keep at it? This one must had knocked you off your feet." I reached again for her cheek. She let me gingerly touch the swollen eye.

"I got back up. I told him again I'd do what I wanted as part of my job, and if he ever hit me again, I'd cut his balls off in his sleep." She grinned painfully through the cut lip. "I guess he didn't believe me. He hit me again."

I felt the blood that had been rising in my face approach a full boil. "And you got up again."

She looked down at her scraped knuckles. "Then it really got nasty. I rushed him and hit at him, trying to knee him in the balls. He twisted, so I got him in the thigh, and he started punching hard into my side. I caught him in the mouth . . ." She held up her fist. ". . . then he grabbed this little club thing he takes with him to the garage and smashed my arm and pounded it into my ribs."

"How bad is the arm?"

"He just cracked the top bone—the radius or whatever that is. It's not broken all the way through."

I sat back in the chair. My first thought was that I needed to take her home with me. Let her use the spare room until she could find another place to stay. But I realized just as quickly that being at my place would be used by that asshole as proof he had reason to be jealous. I went to the door and called to Doc Waterman and Joseph, then sat again in front of my battered deputy.

"I'm going to ask Officer Joseph if you can stay with her for a few days. I know you don't like the idea, but it gets you out of town. I also know you well enough to know you'll want to be doing something. We can have you calling people who were at the hotels and, if the Doc agrees, have you pick up the tapes and watch video of the parking areas."

She shook her head firmly. "You're right. I won't go up there, even if she'll take me."

"Then give me a better idea."

"I can stay at the Super 8 and come to the office to call people."

"Not acceptable. If you're in town, you won't be safe." Joseph followed Doc Waterman back into the examination room. Before Grace could object again, I stood and turned to the state investigator.

"Do you think you could put Grace up for a few days? I think she needs to be out of reach until this cools down."

Joseph looked quickly over at the glowering deputy, then back at me with a flash in her eyes that didn't suggest complete enthusiasm. Either the tension between the women was greater than I realized, or she'd been looking forward to a night at my place more than she was letting me know. But the glint disappeared as quickly as it had come. "Of course, I can," she said. "I'm about ready to head back up that way." She turned to Grace. "Are you feeling up for a drive?"

"I can find a place here," Grace grumbled, letting the spark remain in her eyes as she glared at me.

Joseph stepped forward and looked seriously at the battered woman. "You know Tate's right, Grace. You need to get out of town for a few days—and be someplace this guy doesn't know about." She tossed her head toward the door. "Come on. Let's get going so we don't get up there too late."

"Before you go," I interrupted, "could you make a visit with me? Doc, can you stay here with Grace for another twenty minutes? We shouldn't be long."

He nodded. "I want to check a few more things before I let her go anyway."

The peeling clapboard house was four blocks from the clinic. We walked, avoiding the alert a patrol car would give if it pulled up in front. And I needed time to cool to a simmer. I knocked sharply while Joseph stood tucked in close against the doorframe, out of view of the front window.

"What do you want?" Sal yelled through the door.

"Open up," I called back. "We need to have a talk."

"I got nothing to talk to you about."

"You've got plenty to talk to me about, Sal. Open the damn door before I break it in."

"I've got a gun, Tate. You've got no right to be coming in here.

You come through that door, and I'll blow your damn head off."

I glanced over at Joseph who was unsnapping the strap on her weapon. "I've got every reason to come in, Sal. You've assaulted Grace."

"Maybe she assaulted me," he shouted. "Maybe I'm the one needs to be charging her with something."

"Then open the door and do it," I snapped back. "And just so you don't decide to get stupid, there are two of us out here, both armed. So put the gun down."

There was silence for a moment, then the door inched open. Joseph stayed pressed along the wall. "I don't see nobody else," Sal growled.

"I'm here," Joseph said sharply.

Sal pulled the door far enough inward to allow him to crane his head around to bring her into view. She had her firearm pressed against her hip.

The young Latino's lip was split and swollen, his left cheek deeply bruised with the color running up into his eye. Grace had landed one hell of a blow—or more. He held a 9 mm Glock up against the swelling.

"You see this? This is what that cheating bitch did to me. And you should know why." Joseph raised her weapon and centered it on Sal's forehead.

"You better lower that thing very slowly off to the side," I said. "Officer Joseph here is the woman who shot LJ Greaves. She can get a little trigger happy if a gun gets pointed at someone she's with."

Sal slowly lowered his weapon, his glare showing the same rage he had unleashed on Grace.

"Put it on the table there," I ordered, nodding at a side table beside the door. Sal hesitated long enough for Joseph to extend her weapon menacingly, then lowered it to the tabletop.

"Okay," I said through the screen. "You listen to me, you son of a bitch. Grace works with me. That's it. As part of our work we sometimes go places together. That's it." I leaned into the screen. "But I will tell you this. She's an important part of my team. And I promise you that if you *ever* so much as threaten her again, I'll come back over here and kill you. Do you understand what I'm telling you, you big prick? I don't mean I'll beat the shit out of you. I'll goddamn kill you. Are we clear?"

Sal blinked hard, his jaw tightening. "You threatening me in front of a cop?"

I shook my head slightly. "Not threatening. Promising. And I can also promise that if something happens to you, Officer Joseph here will deny she ever heard anything."

Sal glared sullenly at the two of us but said nothing. I jabbed a finger into the screen.

"You got that, Sal? Never, *ever* touch Grace again." I turned and walked down the three concrete steps. Joseph stood long enough to give the man her own confirming look, then backed away.

When we heard the door slam behind us, she holstered her weapon and looked over at me. "That was a pretty risky threat. He might tell people. You better hope nothing happens to the guy in the next while."

"If something does, it may very well have been me. It was all I could do to keep from beating the shit out of him tonight."

"That's quite a commitment to your deputy."

"I'd do the same if it were you," I muttered, and we walked the rest of the way to the clinic in silence.

14

On the second day of her sequester, Grace Torres packed up her few belongings and left Joseph's apartment without notice.

"She's being good to me, but she really doesn't want me there," she announced when she showed up at the office at 9:00 on Friday morning. The purple splotches on her face were beginning to fade and yellow around the edges.

"Sure, she wants you there," I argued. "She wouldn't have asked you to come if she didn't want you there."

"She didn't ask," Grace retorted. "You asked her for me."

"And why wouldn't she want you there?"

Grace dropped her duffle onto a chair and a thick folder onto her desk. She stood looking at me as if I didn't have a brain in my head. "Sometimes . . .," she began, glancing over at Marti, but didn't complete the sentence.

I waited. No more comment. "Well, you can't go back to Sal. You'd better go stay with your parents."

"Not a chance," she muttered. "I'll stay out at the Super 8 until I can find a place."

Marti had been running copies and dropped a pile of duplicated reports on her desktop. "We've got a spare room. You can stay with us," she offered. "I was going to suggest that to begin with, but Tate had already talked to Joseph." She cast me a cynical frown. "I didn't see how that was going to work."

Grace started to protest, but Marti waved her concern away. "Just come home with me after work. We'll set you up for as long as you want to stay."

Grace gave her a grateful nod, opened her folder without sitting, and turned to business. "I pretty well eliminated the people on our call lists. But I started to watch the parking lot video yesterday and there's something I think might be good." She handed me five sheets of paper with car descriptions and license numbers neatly listed in two columns. A white, late-model Mercedes Sprinter box truck was highlighted in yellow in several places on every page.

I glanced over the sheets, resisting the urge to change my morning plan and get right on this. That damned obsession. I laid them back on Grace's folder.

"Tug Divine's memorial's this morning," I said, glancing over at the wall clock. 9:30. "It starts at ten and won't last long, but I'm worried there won't be many there. I want Matt to know how much I appreciate him doing the service for the old man. Marti's going with me, and D'Amico's meeting us there. You want to come along?"

She shook her head. "Not looking like this."

I nodded my understanding, unbuckled my weapon, and waited for Marti to grab her jacket. We left Grace with her files and turned up 2nd Street toward the gray stone church with its twin Norman belfries that stood at the corner of Madison. Marti chuckled under her breath.

"I don't think you're going to have to worry about a crowd, Tate," she said. Ahead of us, most of Crayton was lined up at the church's high wooden doors, waiting patiently to join in a community remembrance of their mail carrier who couldn't resist the bottle. By the time we made it into the sanctuary, it was standing room only against the back wall. Three rows ahead of us, the Haddad clan filled a full pew. I wondered if they had even heard of Tug Divine before news of his death appeared in the *Daily*, or just felt like being there was part of being a good church citizen.

As I'd guessed, the service was short. *Amazing Grace* sung by Carol Langley, a short obituary read by David Masterson, who had been postmaster when Tug was walking his route, and ten minutes from Reverend Frazee. There was no mention of hellfire and about as little of heaven. Matt focused on the acts of kindness Tug had done for people as he walked the streets of town. Returning a lost kitten. Dropping his carrier bag on a porch to clear a walk for Mrs. Briarson after an unexpected snow. Taking ten minutes to console Denise Wallace when he realized, as he reached the end of her walk, that the letter just delivered told her of the passing of a cousin who had been a close friend and playmate when they were girls.

"Tug's passing has reminded me of two important lessons," Matt said as he wrapped up. "The first is that each of us has our weaknesses. Some more visible than others. We should never allow our awareness of them in others to cause us to overlook or forget the good and the kindness they brought into our lives. And the second lesson—as much to me as to anyone else here—is that we should never be a community that allows a man who has been our friend and supporter to die alone in the woods because he didn't have someone to help him make it home. I'll be forever grateful to Tug for those two reminders."

Around me, the people of Crayton nodded and sniffled and, as Carol sang *I'll Fly Away*, we all committed to be better supporters of each other.

"This van was parked in the lot every day Farid Sayegh was at the Hampton," Grace said when we were again gathered around her desk. "It left the day he stopped showing up at the hotel. The desk has no record of the van being registered to anyone who was checked in. It's a Mississippi plate. Joseph had her office trace the number for me. It's registered to a Jason Anzar who lives in Brandon."

I looked through the dates recorded beside each highlighted van entry. In some cases, the Sprinter had moved three or four times during the day. "This is good work, Grace. And what do we know about Jason Anzar?"

She lowered herself gingerly into her desk chair and punched her computer's "on" button. "I just got the report from the state police last evening," she grumbled. "That's why I'm here this morning."

"We can run this down. You need to give those ribs a few more days to heal."

She sniffed. "My ribs are fine. It's my brain that's starting to turn to mush. I need to be working at more than calling business people who happened to be at the Hampton for four nights."

I waved the parking list in front of her. "This supports the theory you had earlier, and it's the best lead we've had in a week. All your work."

"Well," she said defiantly, "now I'm ready to chase that lead from here at my desk."

Mara Joseph pushed through the street door, gave each of us a quick look, and settled on me and the sheets in my hand, saying nothing about Grace's departure.

"I see you've been talking about the van. Rosario called about half an hour ago with something that could be another break. He thinks he may know where the explosives came from."

I nodded toward the door to the fishbowl. "Grace, why don't you join us in the inner sanctum?"

As Joseph crossed to my office, Grace detoured by Marti's desk and handed her a slip of paper with Jason Anzar's name and hometown written on it. "If you're tired of filing, maybe you could run this through social media and see what we can learn about our Mr. Anzar. Then check to see if he's got a record anywhere." Marti took the paper with a relish that suggested she'd been hoping something might bring a little variety to her morning.

In my office, I plopped behind the scarred oak desk that was one of the few carryovers from the old bank. "What have you got?" I asked Joseph when we were all settled. She had managed to beat Grace to the corner chair. Grace chose to perch beside the door rather than accept one of the fold-outs.

Joseph spoke as if I were the only other person in the room, leading me to wonder what the hell had been going on at Casa

Joseph the last two days?

"The Bureau's been able to trace the explosive that was used at the dam site," she announced. "That particular pack was made up of blocks of what the Army calls M112, which is basically C4. These blocks were part of batches that had been 'repurposed' in 1999 at one of three munitions plants: one in Iowa and two in Tennessee." She paused to see if I had questions, still keeping her eyes focused across the desk. I gave her a quick nod to go on.

"Each of these three plants has stored some of the material and sent some to training and deployment sites around the world. The Bureau began by having the three depots run inventories on their stored material. The Iowa plant came up half a dozen units short."

"That stuff must be carefully guarded," I observed. "How would someone get six bags that size out of the depot?"

"Rosario and two other agents are there now. It's somewhere up near Burlington, if you know where that is. Southeast part of the state along the Mississippi. The place is under video surveillance twenty-four seven. They seem to know exactly where the missing units were stored, and it was covered all day, every day, by cameras. They're going through the backup video, and he hopes he'll know something by tomorrow."

Grace spoke from beside the door, forcing Joseph to glance her way. "As much as I dislike the Greaves, I still think it's highly unlikely they were able to get ahold of the stuff. No good way to contact anyone who had it."

Any reply from Joseph was cut short by Marti, who stepped into the room, looking around importantly. "Pardon the interruption, but I found your man Jason Anzar. He's on Facebook, living in Brandon, Mississippi." She paused dramatically. "And get this. It looks like he recently left the service where he was with the 155th Armored Brigade Combat Team. His last deployment before being discharged? Northern Syria."

15

Two huge breaks on our dead Syrian case and both frustrating as hell. What they did, basically, was move the investigation out of the county and into the hands of the Feds. Rosario was chasing down the missing demolition packs. Joseph's call to the Bureau about Jason Anzar pretty well put that piece of the puzzle in their hands as well. That left our department with the routine and much less engaging job of keeping the locals safe from each other and from the ravages of distracted driving and drug use.

Frankie was finally able to nail Ernest Bonebrake for speeding without a license and without his seatbelt fastened. Ernie weighs in at about four hundred pounds. He's notorious in the county for taking his wife Jan's little Ford Fiesta for a five-mile, LeMans-style sprint from his place out on Highway MM to the Sonic for a Route 44 super-sized drink, two bacon double cheeseburgers, and an order of mozzarella sticks. He has a pickup of his own. But it seems to be a lot easier to throw his bulk behind the wheel of the Fiesta with the seat full back, lower the wheel against his massive belly, and gun the Ford along the two-lanes that wind through the farms and timberland into town. Any unsuspecting motorist who dares to try to share the road risks being forced onto the shoulder or, in his most aggressive moments, into a drainage ditch.

Ernie has been driving without a license for nearly two years now but isn't at all deterred by any sense of wrong-doing. On this fateful day, he'd forced Ritter off the road on a tight turn on Cloverhill Road and had enough sense not to try to outrun the deputy on the milelong straightaway that followed.

The way Frankie told the story—waiting until the evening crew had come in and he had a full audience—he could see Ernie fumbling with the seatbelt as he approached the vehicle. Frankie waited until Bonebrake rolled down his window, then said, "Ernie, what are we going to do with you? Driving like a maniac in this tin can of a car. No license and no seatbelt."

"You nailed me, Rambo," Ernie confessed, holding up his hands in mock surrender. "But you can't get me for no seatbelt."

"'Hell I can't!' I told the dumbass," Frankie recounted with more than his usual display of drama. "I pointed at his belt. He's so damn fat that when he tried to buckle up in a hurry, he looped it through the steering wheel. Couldn't have made the next turn without driving off the road. I got a picture of it, and we'll see what Judge Werner does with him this time. We may have to put a tracking collar around one of them hambones of an ankle. Then, when it starts to move, we'll know Ernie's back on the road."

We all knew Werner wouldn't throw Ernie in jail but would give him a fine and order him again to stay off the roads if behind the wheel. Janet would do her best to keep him home and on whatever diet she's trying to force on the man. Then the siren call of bacon double cheeseburgers and an Oreo cheesecake shake would overpower poor Ernie and he'd violate his probation.

Grace was committing her quiet days in the office to seeing what more she could learn about Jason Anzar. Though the Bureau laid claim to him now, she needed something that would keep her body sedentary and her mind kicked into investigative gear.

"Werner will fine him again," she mumbled from her desk. "And that's probably the right thing to do. A few weeks in jail won't change him, and we can't afford to feed him. We just need to get his place wired to the tornado sirens so when he heads for town, Jan can sound the alarm. Three short bursts will mean the world needs to stay clear of MM."

"He'll kill himself one of these days," I offered. "Hope he doesn't take anyone with him."

"I ain't covering *that* wreck," Frankie groused. "It'll look like someone blew up the rendering plant." The image brought a quick halt to the Ernie Bonebrake seatbelt discussion.

I used the light afternoon to take a half-day to begin resealing the siding on my house. It was a balmy seventy degrees outside, with low humidity for a change. Perfect for brushing oil-based stain on red cedar. The house is pretty basic: two bedrooms and two baths along the back. An open kitchen-dining area separated by a waist-high bar from a great room in what I call the front, even though it opens onto a deck that extends to the south out over the edge of a timbered slope that drops away to the creek below. Beyond that, forty acres of pasture flood just often enough to keep anyone from putting barns or chicken houses on it. The house sits on sixteen acres of hardwoods about a quarter mile down a gravel lane, with no neighbors in sight in any direction. All good from my point of view and just what Joseph finds so appealing about the place.

I'd built the house with the help of the guy who had been my building trades teacher when I took a few afternoon classes at the regional tech school that serves six school districts down here along the Arkansas line. By the time I came back to Crayton, Clarence had retired and was willing to hire on as my project manager and construction guru. Between the two of us, we did all but pour the slab and finish the drywall, jobs Clarence said he was too old to do and didn't have the patience to try to coach me through. One of his warnings before returning to his stress-free life was to re-apply a semi-transparent stain to the siding every two years.

"If you want a gray house, don't worry about it," he said. "If you want it to look like cedar, brush it down with soap and water and a stiff bristle brush every couple of years, then re-seal. No wire or steel wool, or you'll get dark splotches where metal fibers stick in the wood. Just a good, stiff bristle brush, rinse it down, and let it dry well before you seal it." It was time for a new coat of sealer.

A mindless task like brushing wood siding has all the advantages of a long drive on a freeway when there's no semi traffic. Hours with the task at hand on cruise control and the mind wandering. I started along the west side of the house where the afternoon sun had done the most fading, thinking I'd work my way around onto the deck where I could use the patio lights to keep going after dusk. Plus, two thirds of the wall on the deck side is window. Once I turned the corner, I should be able to make good headway and feel like I was getting a lot done the first day.

As I scrubbed, I tried to fit together the puzzle pieces that had been handed me since I'd been jarred awake by the dam explosion and the discovery of Sayegh's body. The question that still ate at me like a dug-in deer tick was whether the two events were connected. Did whoever blew up the dam know a body was buried there?

On the one hand, it seemed unlikely that anyone would go to the trouble of burying a body, only to blow it back into the air a few days later. On the other hand, what were the chances that someone would manage to get a contraband military demolition pack, blow up the burial place of a man who had come into the country illegally to assassinate some Syrian refugees, and the two not be connected in some way? Pretty damn slim, it seemed to me. I moved my ladder six feet to the right, refilled my bucket with warm, soapy water, and attacked the next section of paneling with my bristle brush.

Only a fool would try to use twelve blocks of C4 without knowing what they were doing. That was enough explosive to bring down a good-sized building. Jason Anzar had been in an Army armored division and had shown up in the Hampton parking lot, but not in the Hampton Inn, at the same time Sayegh had been killed. Then, Anzar had disappeared from parking security tapes the next day. But if he was there to kill Sayegh, how did he know the Syrian was in the country when the FBI's counterterrorism unit didn't? And why would he go to the trouble of burying his victim, then blow him out of the ground with such a huge charge, just to have the body discovered?

As I reached the corner that turned across the deck wall, light was beginning to fade into a muted orange behind the oaks to the west, and a theory was beginning to form in a dim corner of my brain. Anzar had been following Sayegh. Someone *else* had been following Anzar and wanted his work exposed, including the fact that the Syrian had been buried in the dam.

The tick burrowed a little deeper, itching where I couldn't scratch. I brushed my way across the top of the windows that now reflected the deck lights against a dark interior. Why would whoever was following Anzar want to make certain Sayegh was found? To lead to Anzar? To send a message back to the dead man's family that their assassin had failed, been killed, and unceremoniously disposed of? The desecration would be as grave an affront to Sayegh's family as the killing. This last thought stopped my stiff bristle brush in mid-stroke. No one would want to send that message more than the Haddad brothers. Maybe the Feds had taken over, but this mess had just fallen right back into my own lap.

My cell buzzed in my hip pocket. The display read "Marti." I stepped down from the short ladder and dropped the brush into my bucket.

"Hi, Marti. What's up?"

In the background, I heard pounding and the slurred baritone of a man shouting.

"Tate. You need to get over here as fast as you can." Marti's voice was a panicked cry. "Nolan's not home, and Sal's trying to break in to get to Grace. He's got a gun with him, and she's got hers out. One of them's going to kill the other if he gets through the door."

I was on my way through the house before she could finish the sentence. Marti and her husband farm four hundred acres of corn and soybeans a mile north of town. Their house sits back off the road in a grove of ancient walnut trees, far enough from neighbors that a shot wouldn't be heard.

"Easy, Marti," I said, trying to calm her panic as I fought to control my own. "Call Larry and Bobby. See if either's closer, and get them over there. I'll be about ten minutes."

"Larry's up north by Taylorville," she whispered against the pounding on the door. "I called him first. He's started this way. But he'll be at least half an hour. I can't raise Bobby. He must be in one of the dead zones."

I swept the keys and my sidearm from the hook beside the back door and sprinted toward the Explorer, the phone still clutched in one hand. "Keep him out as long as you can. I'll run with the siren on. Maybe I can scare him off."

"Hurry," she begged. "He's threatening to shoot us both."

The route between my place and Marti's is a winding, tree-lined ribbon along a ridgeline that drops down into a patch of farmland northeast of town, divided by narrow gravel roads that run at right angles with the section lines. My drive over would have impressed even Ernie Bonebrake. On the way, I voice-dialed Dave Johansson, the state patrolman assigned to the Crayton area, pulling him away from dinner.

"Dave, there's an active shooter at the Bleasdale farm. He's after Grace Torres who we have staying there after the guy beat her up. Do you have an officer on duty in the area? I may need some help."

"On my way," Dave said. "It'll be about twenty minutes."

I could see the lights of the old family farmhouse across a field of soybeans a half-mile away. If Salvador was still trying to break in, he should hear the wail of the siren and see the flashing red and blue of the light bar.

As I wheeled the Explorer into Marti's drive, the rear passenger and drivers-side windows shattered as I heard the sharp report of a handgun. Sal Becerra stood unsteadily on the lighted porch, waving a blocky pistol in my direction. I spun the patrol car off the drive behind two of the giant walnuts and bailed from the car behind one of the trees. I was still fifty yards from the house.

"Sal, put down the gun," I shouted across the darkening expanse of lawn. A second shot took the sideview mirror off the Explorer.

"Damn it, Sal! I don't want to have to shoot you, you stupid sonofabitch. Put the gun down, and let's talk this over."

"You think my woman's your *puta*?" he yelled back, firing a shot that barked the tree beside my shoulder. "You saved me hunting you down. I'll kill you here, then she'll wish she'd never let you touch her."

"There's nothing going on between me and Grace," I called back. "You're going to get yourself a life sentence over nothing." His response was another round that whined past the tree without hitting anything. Four shots. I guessed the weapon to be the Glock 19 he'd threatened us with at his house, which meant a fifteen-round magazine. If he hadn't fired before I got there, he still had eleven rounds. There wasn't time to try to run him out of ammunition. His firing was erratic, but I'd be just as dead if hit by an erratic bullet. Sucking in a deep breath, I broke from behind the tree, zig-zagging to the next closest trunk. The effort drew two more shots but put me thirty yards from the porch.

I hadn't shot at a man since Iraq. When I ran for sheriff, I knew it would always be a possibility, but one I hoped I could do the job well enough to avoid. This wasn't looking promising. Grace had been on the force for three years before I was elected, and the gossip had stayed pretty low key until I appointed her chief deputy. Everyone agreed that of the people we had, she was the right choice. Smart. Tough. Decisive. Well-trained. If she'd been male or homely as a box of rocks, no one would have given it a second thought. But a lot of the men in the county couldn't imagine working side-by-side with someone who looked like Grace without making a move on her. And a lot of the women suspected the men they knew were thinking just that. The only thing that kept speculation from running rampant was Grace's relationship with the asshole who now had me pinned behind a walnut. I knew if I shot the bastard, the rumor mill would go ballistic.

The siren of Larry Newby's cruiser wailed across the night-shrouded field of soybeans, the red of his light bar dotting the horizon.

"Sal, backup's coming," I called from behind the tree. "You can't take us all on. Put the weapon down, and don't make things worse for yourself." I dropped prone and peeked around the base of the trunk. Sal had stooped into a crouch behind a flimsy rail post, squinting in the light of the porch at the approaching squad car.

Newby swung into the drive, spotted my Explorer, and wheeled left to flank the shooter. He swung around to blast the porch with his headlights, threw open the driver's door, and crouched behind it.

"Stay low," I shouted. "He's taken six shots at me and won't put down the weapon."

Larry had twenty years with the Springfield PD before moving to private security work for Jack Henry. He's pretty well seen it all and isn't rattled by anything.

"Sal. Better give up on this before you get yourself killed," he yelled over the car door. Sal's answer was a frantic shot that blew out one of Newby's headlights.

"Can you get to that tree closer in on your right?" Larry called in my direction. "I'll give you cover."

"Okay. *Now!*" I jumped to my feet and sprinted for the lone oak in the front yard, a towering red oak with a trunk as thick as a whiskey barrel. Larry covered with two quick shots, both of which were returned in his direction. I rolled behind the tree and flattened against the trunk.

"Time to put the gun down," I yelled at Sal. "Larry, I'm going to give him a three count. You ready over there?"

No response from Newby.

"You okay, Larry?" More silence.

"Newby? Give me a shout if you're alright over there?" No answer.

From the porch, I heard another shot smash into the lock plate on the door. I bolted to my feet, spinning from behind the oak into a low crouch, weapon extended. Sal had stepped back and was about to drive a heel into the shattered door lock.

"*Becerra,*" I shouted.

He spun, eyes flashing red in the beam of Newby's single headlight. The tree beside my face shattered into wood shrapnel. My shot caught him square in the chest, throwing him back against the broken door and splattering it crimson. Sal hung for a brief moment against the stained wall, then pitched sideways onto the porch.

16

If the county commissioners had had their way, there would have been no investigation. Sal Becerra had a reputation as a mean, hot-tempered S-O-B who liked to pick on anyone he thought he could push around. Especially women. People couldn't understand what Grace saw in the guy or why she'd put up with him for nearly two years. Word spread fast around Crayton that he'd beaten her pretty badly. Outside of the office, Marti Bleasdale is generally as tight-lipped as a Carmelite nun. But in this case, she made it her personal mission to pass along vivid descriptions of the thirty minutes of terror that led up to Sal's shooting. Still, there had to be an investigation. Someone, in their infinite wisdom, had written an "officer-initiated shooting" procedure into our departmental bylaws.

I was just smart enough to know that I ignored any policy at my own peril. Able Pendergraft, who'd practiced law in Crayton since before Grace was born, had written every will in town and had served as legal counsel for ten thousand minor offenses, wouldn't have touched a lawsuit against me. And Judge Werner would have thrown it out as baseless. But I knew some young Springfield attorney might see the shooting incident in the *News-Leader*, smell an officer abuse case, and come after me. He'd demand a change of venue to Greene County, try to select a jury of folks who'd had some run-in with the law, and turn Sal into a victim. Give the case a "Sheriff Shoots Lover's Boyfriend" spin. My only protection was a thorough investigation.

Dave Johansson had wheeled into the drive while I was still crouched over Larry Newby, trying to stem the bleeding from a shoulder wound that had knocked him all the way to the back of his patrol car. Grace had come out onto the porch, taken a panicked look at the two downed bodies, and fallen back into an old rocker, clutching her knees and staring at Sal while Marti stroked her back. I glanced up as Dave came around the back of Newby's cruiser carrying his service weapon and a powerful flashlight. He was dressed in civvies.

Dave knelt beside the deputy. "How bad is he?"

I pressed a wad of gauze from Newby's first aid kit hard against his shoulder. "He's unconscious, but alive. He's lost a lot of blood. When he didn't answer me, I thought he was dead. But it looks like the door may have knocked him out. The shot hit the frame and ricocheted into Larry, slamming the window bar back into him." I pointed at a long red welt across his forehead that was quickly darkening to purple.

"Have you called an ambulance?"

The distant scream of a siren answered his question.

"Chase is on his way. He and his wife were having dinner at Waterman's, so I think the doc is with him." With one bloody hand, I reached to my hip and handed Dave my Sig. "Sal's on the porch. You better go look the scene over and get some pictures while Chase runs Larry to the hospital. He can come back for the body later and take Sal to Springfield."

Johansson stood and looked from Newby to the porch. "You sure Sal's dead?"

"Pretty sure. I hit him in the middle of the chest."

"And he shot Newby?"

I glared at him across the fallen man, but knew it was a question he had to ask. "Sal got off eight or ten shots. Six at me, and a couple at Larry. I was over across the yard behind that oak and figured Larry'd been hit when he didn't answer. Then, when Sal shot the lock out of the front door, I had to take him down."

Dave turned and waved the approaching ambulance over to the patrol car. "Did you warn him before you shot?"

"Over and over. Marti and Grace were inside and could hear everything. They can tell you how it all went down."

Grace had pushed suddenly from the rocker, stepped around her fallen boyfriend, and rushed from the porch as if she'd just become aware that Newby was down. She dropped onto her knees beside him, joined by Doc Waterman, as Chase pulled the rolling stretcher from the rear of the ambulance.

Grace grasped the deputy's limp hand, looking at me pleadingly. "I'm so sorry, Tate," she sniffled. "This is all my fault. Is Larry going to be alright?"

The doctor pulled my dressing away from the wound, slid a hand under Larry's back to see how much the bullet had spread, then waved us back to clear a path for the stretcher. "I don't think it hit any bone," he guessed. "He's lost a lot of blood, but not enough to be critical. I think he'll make it. We need to get some fluids in him." He pointed up at the bruised swath just above Newby's nose. "What happened here?"

I stood and fingered the crease on the inside edge of the window frame. "The way I see it, the shot kicked the door back hard into him as it glanced into his shoulder. The combination knocked him out."

Doc Waterman grunted and helped lift the deputy onto the cart. "I'm not sure he got hit by the whole bullet. Not that much spread. Any reason I need to check on the other victim?"

"Either you or Chase needs to pronounce him dead at the scene," I suggested. "I don't see any reason to move the body until Chase gets back and, for the record, it would be good to make it clear we didn't need to be rushing him to the hospital."

"Chase," the doctor called to the ambulance owner. "You're the coroner. Why don't you go make sure we don't have another live one we need to transport before we leave. I'll work on this wound."

Dave Johansson took Grace's hand and lifted her to her feet. "Are you okay, Torres? Would you like me to take you somewhere to be checked over?"

Grace folded her arms tightly across her chest and shook her head mutely.

"Let me walk you through how this all happened for your report, Dave," I offered. "I'll stay here with Sal until Chase gets back and can take him up to the morgue."

"You gonna be alright, Tate?" he asked.

I nodded, still feeling my pulse thumping a few beats above normal, but without a shred of guilt about having taken down Sal Becerra.

A second state patrol car sped toward us along one of the section lines. "That'll be Mike Holland," Dave said. "He's the duty officer tonight. I'm going to let him walk you through everything and file the report so it's official. I'll add what I can tomorrow." He handed my weapon back. "Give this to Mike. Then, I suggest you call Bobby Lule. As of now, you're on suspended leave, and Grace is in no shape to take over."

We had no internal "shooting team" in the department and, even if we had, half of us were either the shooter, the intended victim, or in the hospital. The investigation fell to the state patrol and, to my relief, into the hands of Mara Joseph. It wasn't that I was worried about being exonerated. I knew it was a clean shoot, made under fire, and with two innocents in immediate mortal danger. Every possible warning had been given to the deceased. But internal investigations have a way of being unpredictable, of dragging on for weeks, and can be a complete pain in the ass. We didn't have time for a sideshow, and I didn't have the patience to be jacked around by an inquest when the facts were so clear. Joseph would do her job, and would do it quickly.

I'd stayed at the scene until Chase came back for the body, made sure Grace would be alright with Marti and Nolan, then driven over to the Newby place. Larry's wife, Tammy, needed to hear from me that he'd been shot, but would be okay. I ended up staying for nearly an hour while she pulled herself together and called a neighbor to drive with her up to the medical center. By the time I got ahold of Rocky D'Amico to tell him half the department was out of service and he was in charge of the day shift until I got cleared, it was 3:00 a.m. I vaguely remember driving home.

Joseph called at 10:00, just as I was rolling out after six hours of restless tossing.

"Can you meet me at the Bleasdale place at 11:00?" she asked. "I'd like to get this investigation out of the way as soon as we can, and it needs to start with you. I have Officer Holland's report which looks pretty straight forward, but would like to take a look at the scene with you before we have other interviews."

I reached Marti's house five minutes before the hour and found Joseph there with a young state trooper named Owens who had been assigned to be the other part of the shooting team. I recreated the scene while both took notes and snapped pictures.

"I have Newby's weapon," Joseph said. "He fired two rounds. Are you sure it was you who hit Becerra and not Newby?"

I pointed at the gash in the porch siding, now scrubbed a washed pink, but not repaired. "Larry was firing cover shots while I ran for the oak," I said. "He wouldn't have been trying to bring Sal down, but keep him from firing at me. If you check the angle of the shot that went through Sal and into the wall, you'll see it came from my position over there. And dig out the slug. It will be from my Sig."

She sent Evans to the porch to confirm my explanation. When he was out of earshot, she turned away from him and said, "This all looks clean, Tate. But I want you to stay away from the office until you get a call from me to come in. We met with Larry this morning. He's doing pretty well and his story corroborated yours exactly. We're leaving here to talk to Grace and Marti in town. As long as we don't hear something unexpected, I plan to meet with the commissioners this afternoon and recommend they put you back on the job tomorrow. I've got a couple of new pieces of information you'll be interested to hear. Maybe we could meet this evening."

"You met with Larry this morning and didn't say anything

about it?"

"Procedure, Tate. We wanted to hear your account before you knew we'd heard his. Since they corroborate exactly, it makes the testimony stronger."

Evans had satisfied himself on the porch and was headed back toward us.

"Why don't you come out to my place this evening?" I suggested. "It might not look good if we have a casual get-together in town the day of the investigation."

"I'll call you," she said and moved away to meet with the patrolman.

17

The last time Mara Joseph had been to my house, we'd spent the night together. We had just returned from our investigative trip to Mexico where we'd been tempted but resisted because we were on business and because we weren't both supposed to be there. On the off chance we'd bump into someone who knew one of us, we wanted to be able to say honestly that it hadn't been a rendezvous. Maximum deniability. The truth was that she thought it wasn't a smart thing to do, and I didn't feel like I could pressure her into changing her mind. We'd both been in recovery at the time: me, from the loss of Adeena, a death that I felt responsible for. Joseph, from a work-related romance that had turned sour. But somehow, during our post-Mazatlán rehash at my place, we had decided our recovery would benefit from some renewed intimacy.

What had started as a "Why don't you use my spare room so you don't have to drive back to Springfield tonight," had turned into a "Let's enjoy each other's company and see if this feels right." To me, it felt perfect. She had immediate regrets. Something to do with "once bitten, twice shy" and not wanting personal complications to get in the way of that requested transfer to St. Louis.

When she called shortly after 6:00 p.m., I'd just finished scrubbing down the kitchen side of the house and the back of the garage with my bristle brush and was thinking about reheating some spaghetti and marinara sauce left over from the weekend.

"Good news," she announced. "Officer Evans and I both concluded the shooting was not only justified, but necessary to save lives. We reported to the commissioners this afternoon. They support full and immediate resumption of duties. I'll file my report with the patrol in the morning but wanted to let you know right away."

"That *is* great news. And thank you." I hesitated, then asked, "Are you still planning to come by?"

"If you have time. There are a couple of things we need to talk about."

"Have you eaten?"

"Not yet. If you haven't, I can bring something with me. How about a Casey's pizza?"

"Half supreme and half whatever you like best," I suggested. "I have plenty of beer."

"I'll be there in half an hour."

By the time I cleaned up and set dishes out on the table on the deck, I heard her pull onto the garage pad. As she had when she'd come to the house before, she gave two quick knocks and walked in, the pizza box balanced on one hand.

"Chicken Alfredo on the other half," she announced. "If you don't like it, I'll be glad to take care of my share."

I took the box and led her through the great room and out onto the deck. Sunset had painted the western sky a rich tangerine, and at the bottom of the ridge, the glassy surface of Mill Creek reflected a paler peach. Four white-tailed does grazed their way across the meadow beyond the creek, and barn swallows swooped and darted overhead after evening insects. Somewhere behind us in the woods, a pair of cardinals courted in the twilight.

Joseph stopped a step onto the deck and gazed out over the meadow. "I'd almost forgotten how beautiful it is out here," she murmured reverently. "And peaceful."

I grinned at her across the table. "I've tried to get you back for a reminder."

"You have. And I haven't been good about replying."

I nodded toward one of the chairs, inviting her to sit. "Well, nice to have you back. And thanks again for a quick and positive report. Let's eat and you can tell me what news you have."

I'd turned the table to give two sides an open view of the valley.

We sat with a corner between us as the evening darkened, saying little while we finished a couple of slices and washed them down with the Michelob I'd chilled. She took a long, slow draw on her beer and settled back.

"The Bureau thinks it's found where the C4 came from," she said matter-of-factly. "The ammunition depot in Iowa."

"The place near Burlington?"

She nodded casually, as if we were discussing some tealeaf revelation by the Webber Sisters.

"How much?"

"Six M183 kits."

"Do they know what happened to them?"

She shook her head just as casually, as if her mind was somewhere else. "There's camera surveillance all over that plant. They seem to know what batch it came from and are studying the video since the last inventory was taken."

"And how far back was that?"

"Last month some time. Virtually every vehicle coming in and out of the plant is checked. They're really concerned about someone getting that much out without being detected."

"So, they've no idea yet where it went?"

"No. Not yet. But they seem confident they'll find the person who took it and learn what happened to it."

"Hmm," I muttered, feeling the same relaxing effects of the company, beer, and evening. The sun had dropped far enough to draw most of the color from the west, leaving a deep blue glow that spread from the horizon midway across the arc of the sky. Two planets had appeared. Mars and Venus, I guessed. The call of the cardinals was replaced by the muted hoot of a lone owl. I rose and flipped on the porch lights. When I turned back, she had stretched out in the chair, her head lolled back and eyes closed. I wondered what she would do if I kissed her on the forehead. As I moved back toward the table, she sighed deeply, then pulled herself back upright.

"Two other new bits of information—one good, one not-so-good," she said in the same matter-of-fact tone, taking another sip at her beer. "The Bureau went to the address on Jason Anzar's license in Brandon and he'd checked out. It was a rental, and the landlord said he hadn't renewed this month."

I shook myself quickly back to reality. "No forwarding address?"

She shook her head. "No address, and no responses yet to a nationwide APB on the white Mercedes Sprinter."

I dropped back into my chair and put a foot up on the empty one across from me. "I'm hoping that's the 'not-so-good.' Nothing to work with there."

"The 'good' is that they discovered he had a connection online with a group on the dark web that call themselves The Talismen."

"Is that Talismen with an '*m-e-n*' or an '*m-a-n*?'"

"M-*e*-n."

I took a pull at my own Michelob, then asked, "How did they find the link? Did he leave a phone or computer behind?"

Joseph chuckled. "One of the things I love about you, Tate, is that you immediately think of the questions it took me ten minutes to come up with. But I did ask. He didn't leave anything, but made one careless mistake. The landlord lived in the other half of the duplex he rented and said Anzar had had some Wifi trouble. He came over and asked if he could use the guy's computer just before he split. Based on the time, the Bureau was able to identify the access and followed it to this encrypted site."

"Could they break in?"

"They haven't yet. Some of these encryption systems are apparently pretty good."

"Yeah," I muttered by way of agreement, then sat in silence for a few moments, watching the last reflected light leave the surface of the creek and wondering what she'd meant by "One of the things I love about you."

"He's our man," I said finally. "Anzar killed Farid Sayegh."

Joseph glanced over with a raised brow. "Because of the connection to the dark web?"

"Because of the Talismen."

"You're ahead of me on this one too, Tate. Explain."

"I think the name's taken from talisman. With an *m-a-n*. You know what I mean by a talisman?"

"Well, yes. Like a charm."

"Like a *nazar* . . . the evil eye amulet that's been left with each of these murder victims."

"You think this is some kind of hit squad?"

I shrugged. "The pieces fit. Our man Jason was in Syria. Yusef Haddad is Syrian and was FSA. Farid Sayegh was Syrian and an Assad informant. Yusef executed the oldest of the Sayegh brothers. It looks like Sayegh was here for revenge but got taken out before he could hit his target. We find an amulet in his pocket that's an Arab charm to protect people from evil."

"The pieces may line up, but I wouldn't say they fit," Joseph objected. "It's a bit like having A, D, F, and G, with B, C, and E still missing."

I challenged her with a skeptical tilt of the head. "So what are B, C, and E?"

"B: How do these Talismen know someone is coming to make a hit? C: How do they know when and where they can find this person to intercept? E: How do they coordinate to have someone at the right place to pick up the target and get the job done?"

"All good questions," I admitted, standing and picking up the rest of the pizza. "It's starting to get a little chilly for my blood. Let's finish whatever you want of this inside. We can figure this all out tomorrow. Is the Bureau going to give some of the case up, or are we still too Ozark to help with it?"

"Don't be cynical," she said cynically. "It sounded to me like they're open to any help we can give them."

"Are you going to be back down, now that we have something new to work with? We're pretty shorthanded until Newby's back on his feet." I wasn't going to be the one to suggest a sleep-over.

She stood, gathered up our plates and bottles, and led me back into the house. While I moved the remaining slices onto a smaller dish and got two cold beers from the fridge, she picked up a photo of me with Adeena in front of the Al Fateh mosque in Manama.

"I'm still waiting for some reason to replace those pictures," I teased.

She returned it quickly to the bar that separates the kitchen from the great room and smiled thinly. "I have periods when my resolve gets pretty weak," she admitted. "Tonight's been one of them. But I think you may have a whole new set of issues."

I lifted one of the beers. She shook her head. "No more before I drive home."

I gave a quick nod of resignation. "Then the resolve isn't completely shattered. And what issues are we talking about?"

She leaned with her elbows on the bar. "As long as I've known you, Tate, you've been beating yourself up because you sent Adeena to interpret at that Baghdad hotel while you took the party at the Embassy. It was an understandable decision, but you can't get rid of the guilt. Last night, you took on a whole other load."

I put both bottles back in the fridge and propped against the stainless door, arms folded. "Okay, Dr. Freud. Lay it on me."

"And as long as I've known you, one other thing has been obvious, too. Grace Torres has a serious thing for you, and you find her pretty interesting yourself. I'm not questioning your feelings for me, Tate. But I've always known I was competing for your affection with a woman who could have been cast as Wonder Woman—aside from maybe her bad choice of boyfriends." She leaned farther onto the bar and tucked her folded hands under her chin.

"The only things that kept you two apart, as far as I've been able to tell, were your admirable commitment not to get involved with someone in your department, and her latching onto that worthless Sal. My guess is that she put up with the bum just to keep from having to think about how much she'd rather be with you."

"You're delusional," I protested, knowing she was right about my admiration for Grace and now wondering about the Sal thing.

"Yeah. Me and Marti Bleasdale. She sees it as clearly as I do. I've seen it when I'm in the office."

I stayed planted against the fridge. "*You're* the one I've been trying to entice into a serious relationship."

She tilted her head and gave me a knowing grin. "Like I said, you won't let one develop with a person in the office. But now, that other excuse is gone. And though you did exactly what you had to do in that shooting situation, you're going to feel guilty as hell. You know you've removed the one real obstacle to completely falling for Grace. It's going to be a rough few months, Tate."

I remained quiet as I muddled through what she had said. At least some of it was true. A first twinge of guilt had come as I stood beside Grace while Chase loaded Sal's body into his ambulance. Not guilt at having shot the sonofabitch, but guilt at knowing it was someone I'd always hated to see Grace with. It had grown as I'd left her with Marti that evening and thought how beautiful she was, even when mired in her own guilt and pain and relief. And I knew I was dreading going into the office for the first time after the shooting. Dreading having to face her after killing her steady, dreading receiving her thanks for freeing her of her tormentor, and dreading looking again at that exquisite face and knowing Grace was free. I pushed the thoughts aside. She wasn't the one gazing at me across the wood slab of the bar.

In her own way, Mara Joseph was just as alluring. Pretty. Petite. Hardly statuesque, but trim, sleek, with bright, mesmerizing eyes that missed nothing. Joseph was intelligent, fun, self-assured, and much more familiar with the world beyond Crayton, Missouri than my chief deputy. She understood my passion for languages and was almost as fluent in Hebrew and Spanish as I was in Arabic.

We could comfortably travel the world together and feel right at home in half of it. And she was a tender and passionate lover, something I had to admit I'd thought about with Grace, but never tried to pursue. I awkwardly struggled to put some of those thoughts into words.

"There are a bunch of things I find attractive about you, Mara, that Grace doesn't have." The words were as awkward as my thoughts, and she wasn't convinced.

"Such as?"

"Well, I think we have many more interests in common. Travel. Language. Some of the things you love about city life that I've enjoyed."

She looked about her with a wry smile. "Yet you've got this beautiful place you've said you wouldn't want to leave. I've seen where you grew up out on Huckleberry Ridge, Tate. Your roots are pretty deep in this area. And you seem to forget that Grace speaks Spanish better than I ever will. As my wise father used to say, appreciating other places and things comes with exposure. Grace might appreciate them as much as I do if she had more experience with them."

My irritation forced me away from the fridge to the end of the bar. "You sound like you're trying to talk me out of caring for you. You're the first woman since Adeena I've seriously wanted to spend time with. What I feel is real, and I've tried to let you know that as best I can."

She stepped close enough to take my hand. "I know that, Tate. I also know you're still struggling with how to move on from Adeena. I think you have these same *real* feelings for both me and Grace. Until you can get that sorted out, I'm not sure it's fair for me to influence you in ways she can't, especially now that she's free of Sal. And it's not smart of me to get more involved with you until you have this worked through."

"How noble," I said, more caustically than she deserved.

She ignored the snarkiness. "It has nothing to do with nobility," she said evenly. "I'm just not that far past a relationship of my own that ended when he realized there was someone he loved more than he loved me. I'm not going there again." She squeezed my hand, leaned forward and gave me a sisterly kiss on the cheek, then moved toward the chair that held her jacket and firearm. "I'll check with the Major about helping you out down here if there's more we can do on the Sayegh investigation." At the door, she turned. "You're a wonderful man, Tate. The best I know right now. See where your life is taking you, and maybe someday we'll find we're headed in the same direction."

18

The old saying that there are two things you can count on, death and taxes, should be amended to include a third: Marti Bleasdale being in the office by 7:45 in the morning. That is, of course, unless the first item on the list gets in the way. Otherwise, Marti will pick up the phone when you call at 7:50.

"How's Grace doing?" I asked, thinking I'd better be the concerned boss before offering my excuse for coming in late.

"I think she's okay. Sal didn't have family in the area and didn't ever talk about any. She's worried about some kind of service for him."

I sniffed. "Just like Grace. The guy beat the crap out of her, came looking to kill her, and she's worried about a funeral."

"Tate, be a little sensitive. This is a tough time for her." She paused while I kicked myself for being such a jerk, then said, "She's here. Do you want to talk to her?"

I hadn't counted on Grace also being in before 8:00 a.m.—or being in the office at all today. "Hmm . . . no," I stammered. "I need to talk to her face-to-face when I see her next. And I called to let you know I have a commitment first thing this morning. I'll probably make it by ten, but that's not certain. I'll call when I'm on the way in."

"Do I need to know where you're headed so I can send someone after you if you get in trouble?"

I couldn't stifle a chuckle. "No. This is a pretty safe visit. Grace is still supposed to be on light duty, so save anything that might be too active until I get there, or give it to Ritter."

I drove southwest into the national forest where shortleaf pines took the place of cedars that mix with the hardwoods up around Crayton. The promise of a clear, cloudless day and bright sun couldn't warm away the restlessness that had kept me slumped dumbly in front of the TV watching a late-night rerun of *Roadhouse* until 1:00 am. I then tossed and turned in bed until giving up at 4:00. I brewed coffee and sat out on the deck wrapped in a blanket, begging for a glow in the east that would mean daybreak.

Part of Joseph's attraction, I knew, was that she was available. And a big part of keeping Grace at bay was that she wasn't. Or, at least hadn't been. When I was honest about it, and I'd tried not to be, I had to admit that the "because we work together" was just an effort on my part to force another degree of separation. In fact, work was part of my attraction to Joseph. We both understood the business we were in. Adeena and I had worked together and, in some ways, it had helped us love each other more. We'd laugh at the times we'd changed a translation to keep from insulting some dignitary, or misused words that were different from one Arabic dialect to another. Working together hadn't been all bad.

I couldn't have a relationship with Grace and be her boss, of course. That wouldn't be fair to the other deputies. I'd seen the messes created when problems developed between people at work and a supervisor had a close connection to one of them. And I could imagine situations in which that could happen in our department. Grace thought Ritter was a shooting accident waiting to happen. He called her a *prima donna* with a badge; not sure what that meant, but certain it was an insult. Someday I'd need to step into the middle of one of those spats. It wouldn't be pretty— and much worse if Grace and I had something between us.

But I remembered a time when I'd thought Grace would make a great police chief for Crayton. Ken Prater was within a couple of years of retirement. Grace could keep an eye on things in town. I'd protect the county. As I'd snuggled under the blanket and sipped at warm coffee, waiting for dawn, I realized I'd entertained those fantasies more often than I liked to admit.

Fifty years of regular visitors had created a flattened dirt pull-off at the end of the path I was watching for. Even so, it wasn't much of a path. More like a game trail that disappeared up the hillside into a dense mix of hickory, oak, sassafras, and hackberry. There were no cars waiting. A break for me. I wanted this to be a private reading.

I've never thought of myself as superstitious. But like most everyone I know, I walk around a ladder that's leaning against the house, get a little nervous when a black cat crosses the road in front of me, and lengthen my stride on a sidewalk to avoid stepping on the cracks. My mother's mother, Granny Durbin, was the superstitious one. To her, every sneeze signified something. One for a kiss. Two for a wish. Three for a letter. Four to get better. Something like that. I don't remember exactly how her little rhyme went, but when I sneeze twice, I still can't resist making a wish. Granny was as convinced as she was of the saving grace of the good Lord that if she saw a girl riding a mule, the unfortunate thing would never marry. Mother told me that when she was a girl, she wasn't allowed near one of the beasts. When my father was killed in a logging accident, Granny stopped every clock in the house until after the burial and draped all the mirrors with white cloth to protect against another death during the next year. Not much of that had rubbed off on me, but I still make a point of leaving a house using the same door I entered through. No sense tempting the fates.

That's what was taking me to see the Webber sisters. As I hiked up the hill through the woods, I wondered how much longer the old women would be able to make this trek down to the road to meet Chase when he ran the ambulance out to take the pair to town? One day he'd arrive and they wouldn't be waiting. He would make the climb himself and bring their bodies down. Both would be dead. There was general agreement around the county that one would never die without the other. That's just how they did things.

On this particular morning with the sun playing in lacy patterns on the sides of the old clapboard house, I found the Webber sisters very much alive. They stood waiting on the porch as if one had stepped in front of a mirror: two aged faces painted by the same brush down to the slightest wrinkle. Both wore plain shifts, cut from the same flowered print. One tottered against a right-handed cane. The other gripped hers in her left. Even the gaps in their smiles showed an eerie kind of symmetry.

"Young Mr. Tate," they greeted in unison. Then one, I wasn't certain which, asked, "And how is your mother?"

I smiled awkwardly and told them she'd been gone for a few years now. It was actually five.

Their faces wilted in unison. "I'm so sorry," the other said. "We don't keep up well with everything. And time seems to pass so quickly. But please come in. I believe this isn't an official visit. You have come for a reading." I'd heard people say how unnervingly aware the sisters were, but this was my first taste of that omniscience. It sent a chill down my spine.

"Yes. If I'm not imposing. I've had some worries I hoped you might be able to help with."

The images separated long enough for one to lead through the door, then paired again and walked me to a small, cloth-draped table tucked into one corner of a plain living room. I saw that Grace was right. Whoever had last painted the interior hadn't bothered to move the sofa and two stuffed chairs pushed against the walls. The pale yellow paint traced around them, leaving a dark shadow of each piece on the wall behind it.

"Do you have a favorite tea?" one asked.

"Pardon my asking," I said. "But I know one of you is Ethel and one Edith. Would you mind telling me who is who?"

They both tittered with what sounded like a very light whinny. The left-handed woman raised her free hand. "I'm Ethel," she volunteered. "That's Edith." I made a mental note to remember that the L in Ethel meant "left." I nodded. Now, if they'd just keep their canes in the same hands.

Tea? I had lived in tea-drinking cultures for much of the last ten years and had never really developed a taste for the drink. Either too bitter or sweetened to the point of being saccharine. "Pick something you think I'll like," I suggested, thinking it might provide another test of the women's prescience.

Ethel and Edith grasped the sides of a straight-backed chair and drew it out together, nodding for me to sit. They divided for a moment and moved to their own sides of the table, looked questioningly at each other for a moment, then grinned and said in unison, "Formosan Oolong."

For the first time since I arrived, the two separated by more than a few feet: Edith to lower herself stiffly into a chair beside me and Ethel to the kitchen to heat a kettle and fetch the tea. Edith put a hand on mine as if we were old friends.

"That beautiful Mexican girl who works with you told us you were now sheriff," she said kindly. I was tempted to let her know that Grace had been born here in the county, just as she had, but thought better of it. To Edith Webber, the comment was as innocent as having said, "That pretty Johnson girl . . ."

"Just over two years now," I told her. "I should have been up to see you before now, just to make sure you were both alright. But I check in with Chase, who comes out to take you to town. And with Jerry at the market. They'd let me know if you needed anything."

Edith squeezed my hand. "Nobody bothers us up here. We've got nothing worth being bothered over. Everyone who comes has questions. We do what we can to help."

Ethel returned with a steaming cup, placed it in front of me, and sat across from her sister. The vapor had a mellow smoothness to it that told me I already liked it better than any I'd tried before.

"It's still very hot," Ethel warned. "When it's cool enough, drink all but about a teaspoon-full. Then, holding the cup up by the handle in your left hand, silently ask what you would like to know."

I lifted the cup for a sip but could feel immediately that it would scald my tongue. Lowering it back to the table, I stalled.

"Formosan Oolong. That doesn't sound like a tea you would find at Family Market. Where do you get it?"

"San Francisco," both said together.

I glanced about the room. No computer. And I'd been told the old pair didn't have a cell phone. "San Francisco? How do you order it?"

Ethel answered. "We invite those who come often to bring their favorite teas. It ties the leaves more personally to the person. One of our regulars is very fond of this tea. She orders extra for us. We felt that you might find it to your liking."

I thought about asking about Lilia Haddad's visits, but Grace had already spoken to them about it, and I'd come for another reason. I shouldn't interrupt the mood.

I tried the cup again. "Does it hurt anything if I blow on this?" I asked awkwardly.

The women laughed musically. "Not a bit. Take what time you need."

I didn't have a lot of time and knew that the longer I was away, the more questions I'd get when I reached the office. I sipped until my mouth adjusted to the temperature, then drank down to the last few drops. The tea had a creamy herbal flavor that soothed as it went down. I'd go online when I got back to the office and see if I could order some. Mental note. Formosan Oolong.

"A very good choice," I agreed, lifting the cup to eye level. I formulated the questions that had been haunting my sleep as best I could and concentrated on the porcelain cup, suddenly feeling very foolish. The serious look on the twin faces told me they saw nothing foolish about it at all.

"Now, carefully turn the cup over onto the saucer and leave it there for a moment to let all the liquid drain," right-handed Edith instructed.

I eased the cup over onto the saucer and left it there with all three of us gazing at it expectantly. What had been a "What the hell do I have to lose?" when I'd made the trek up the hill had been changed by the sister's seeming awareness to nervous expectation.

"That is long enough," Ethel announced. "Please turn it back over with your left hand and place it between us, with the handle toward you." I did as I was told. The sisters bent over the small China bowl.

There were long moments of silence during which the Webbers peered together at the scattering of leaves that remained in the bottom, then up at each other as if exchanging telepathic messages, then back at the leaves. They finally both turned toward me in unison, their faces softening sympathetically. Ethel spoke first.

"You have suffered a terrible loss in your life," she said quietly. "Part of what you wish to know is if you will ever be able to get over that loss."

Though I had begun to allow that the sisters may have some powers of clairvoyance, the comment hit me in the gut like a sucker punch. I felt a flush rise on my cheeks and forehead. Could the old women hear my heart? Surely the pounding must be audible. I blinked back moisture from the corners of my eyes and stared self-consciously into the cup.

Edith again touched my arm. "You will never forget, but you will be able to forgive yourself. And there will be new love."

I steepled my hands with thumbs beneath my chin and tried unsuccessfully to keep the tears in check.

Edith Webber squeezed gently. "She would not wish you to carry this guilt," she murmured.

I wondered fleetingly if Grace had said something to them but knew she never would. "Thank you," I sniffled into my hands and felt Ethel touch my other elbow. We sat in silence for two or three moments while I regained composure, with what I can only describe as psychic energy flowing between me and the two women. Removing their hands, they bent again over the cup. I sucked in a deep breath.

"You have also come to ask about this new love," Edith said, smiling.

"You see two paths before you and are unsure which you should follow," Ethel continued, with no interruption in the thought. "The leaves only tell us that you face these two paths. They do not show which you will follow. But one thing is clear. You will not need to choose. The decision will be made for you."

"Made for me?" My heart skipped a beat, triggered by a crushing fear that there would be another disastrous loss. The women again took my elbows and squeezed softly in unison.

"One path joins you together," Ethel said quietly. "The other, we cannot see its end."

19

When I sauntered into the department office shortly after 11:00, no one asked where I'd been—which made me immediately suspicious. For the first half of my drive from Webber's Mountain, I'd fretted over what the sisters meant by, "The decision will be made for you." By the time I reached Jacob's Creek, a wide spot in the road with thirty or forty houses scattered along three short cross streets, I'd decided there was nothing to be gained by trying to guess. Neither of the twins had mentioned death or danger. Neither seemed particularly uneasy. What would be, would be.

But I did need to worry about explaining my morning absence. If I knew Marti and Grace as well as I thought I did, though neither would suggest it to the other, both suspected that Mara Joseph had spent the night and extended her stay into the morning. But as I entered, Marti looked up with a relaxed smile. Grace was at her desk and seemed equally unconcerned. I headed in her direction, thinking it would be wise to begin the rest of the day by asking how she was feeling.

"You have someone waiting," Marti interrupted, nodding toward the fishbowl. Joseph had risen from her chair when I came into the building and now stood watching me through the half-wall window. *Ahh.* That explained Marti's good humor. Obviously no rendezvous with Mara Joseph. The state investigator nodded with a slight smile and waved me toward Grace's desk, seeming to agree that asking after the deputy's wellbeing was the right place to start.

I sat across from her and said as privately as the open office allowed, "I'm so sorry about how things went out at Marti's, Grace."

She looked at me directly, her tightly clasped hands and rigid jaw telling me she was fighting for control.

"I know you had no choice, Tate. You saved us both. Thank you for coming so quickly. And I'm the one who needs to be sorry. Sometimes I can be pretty thick-headed—especially when everybody warned me. Is Larry going to be okay?"

I gave a solemn nod. "I talked to him yesterday. He'll be fine."

"I'd like to go see him, but . . ."

"I know he'd appreciate it," I said. "He doesn't blame you or anyone else. It's part of what we do."

"What about Tammy? I'm not sure I can face her."

"She was there when I called. She doesn't blame you either."

Grace looked down at the desk. "If I'd been smarter, none of this would have happened. Sal would be alive, and you wouldn't have had to go through this investigation."

I wanted to say, "You're right. We all told you," but said what a kinder, more considerate boss would say. "It probably would have happened with someone else, Grace. We'd have been at someone else's door, stopping him from breaking in. Then you might have been in Newby's shoes."

She looked up again, an expression of resolve masking what I read as embarrassment. "I know you'll think this is crazy, but I'm going to arrange a graveside service for him. He's got no family that I know of, and it's not right for there to be nothing for him. He wasn't all bad."

I held her gaze long enough for her to understand I wasn't completely in agreement, then said, "We'll help you with it. I'm sure Bill Latimer will be willing to do something."

"He was Catholic," Grace murmured.

I leaned back, struggling to remain that considerate boss. "There's no priest in town, Grace. If you want anybody to be there, you'd better have it here in Crayton. Bill can do a nice job. And do you think it's going to make any difference to what happens to Sal?" I knew I was edging toward cruel, but I didn't care.

She lowered her eyes again to the desktop, thought for a moment, then said, "No. I guess not. Reverend Latimer will be fine." When she looked back up, the resolve wasn't masking anything. "Officer Joseph is waiting. You'd better see what she wants. She didn't feel like she needed to share it with us."

I reached across and squeezed her hand. Marti gave me an approving nod as I passed her desk. All was right with the world. At least for the next three minutes.

Joseph waved me around my desk and into my seat as if it were her office. She waited until I was comfortably leaning back, looking at her with what I hoped was an "I'm here. We can do business" kind of look.

"How's Grace doing?" she asked.

"As well as can be expected. But I didn't think I'd see you down here this soon. And I'm fairly certain you didn't come to check on Grace." The Sal memorial thing burned like iodine on a skinned knee and the words of the Webber sisters kept echoing in my head. "You see two paths before you and are unsure which you should follow." The path that faced me now was being solicitous, and that added to the burn.

Joseph frowned irritably. "Don't be small, Tate. Of course, I'm concerned about Grace. But you're right. That's not why I'm here." She glanced over her shoulder at the women working behind her in the main office, then leaned toward me over the desk. "There's a new Sayegh in town."

I surged to my feet so forcefully that the desk scraped across the hardwood, drawing alarmed stares from Grace and Marti. "Who the hell's watching him?" I snapped.

Joseph raised a hand to keep me from bolting for the door. "I have two patrolmen on him. A Qasim Sayegh checked into the Arbor Suites south of the city just before midnight. We'd asked hotels to contact us if anyone with that name registered—or someone on a foreign passport who looked Middle Eastern. The clerk called the patrol. We had someone there within ten minutes." She chuckled under her breath. "If he's here to try to get to one of the Haddads, he's not a very experienced assassin. All the Arbor's rooms open to the outside, and there's only one drive in and out of the parking lot. Easy to watch."

I dropped back into my chair with Grace and Marti's eyes locked on me through the glass. "Why didn't you call as soon as you knew this? I need to warn the families."

Joseph was unruffled. "He's an hour and a half from here. That's plenty of time to get them gathered up and covered if he starts to move. And we saw no reason to trouble you or the Haddads until we did some checking. Plus . . ." She glanced through the glass at my officemates. ". . . I've been here for over an hour. Your cell phone is off, and your little team out there didn't seem to feel any need to tell me where you were."

I ignored the sarcasm but had forgotten I'd turned the phone off when I reached the Webbers' cabin. I pulled it out, punching it back to life. "They didn't know. And a Qasim Sayegh showing up in Springfield? What kind of checking do you think you need to do?"

"I called Rosario immediately. He's on his way out. In fact, should be getting here about now. He said he'd rent a car and come down. Qasim has an airport rental. A blue Hyundai. The Bureau's following up on the information he put on the registration. We could all make a pretty embarrassing mistake if we jump the wrong person without cause."

"Or if we let him kill someone because we didn't act quickly enough. This can't just be another coincidence."

"He could be here looking for his brother."

"Probably so. And to do what his brother didn't get done."

"Like I said, Tate," she said irritably. "We have two officers watching the hotel and you haven't exactly been Mister Available this morning."

"Have they checked the hotel lot for a white Mercedes Sprinter?"

"They have. None there. And they've checked registrations at the hotels around for a Jason Anzar—and have checked the lot for other vehicles that don't belong to employees or registered guests. A blank on both."

I nervously clicked the button on the top of a ballpoint. "So, what's the game plan? I don't like the Haddads not knowing there's a possible threat. The families could be scattered around and hard to protect."

Joseph leaned forward and looked at me intently. "Tate, I've got both Johansson and Holland close by and ready to assist. You have Grace, Ritter, and D'Amico. The seven of us should be able to round up the Haddads and get them to a safe place before some guy who checked into a hotel with outside doors can find his way to Crayton and hunt them down. I'd guess if it's one of the Idlib Sayeghs and he's here to do what Farid didn't do, he's come for Yusef."

Her phone pinged and she glanced at the message. "Rosario's headed this way. I suggest we save our powder until he gets here, develop our plan, and not run helter-skelter around the county getting people all worked up and tripping over each other."

She was right, I knew. When we moved on this and got others involved, we needed to know exactly what we were doing. I suspected there were pieces of this already in motion that we didn't even know about. The missing demolition kits. The role the Talismen might have in what was going on. If this was one of the Sayeghs we'd been watching for, did Anzar and his group of watchmen also know he was here? If they did, how did they find out? Were they tracking him now? I stopped punching the button on the pen and dropped it onto the desk.

"Thank you," Joseph muttered.

I sat back again and the women in the outer office relaxed. "If you have no objections," I said testily, "I'd like to call all of my people in for the meeting with Rosario. Deputies Ritter and D'Amico and my night guy, Bobby Lule. I want everyone on board. Any problem with that?"

Joseph smiled thinly, suggesting that she didn't feel she

deserved the biting tone. "No objection from me. And I'd think Agent Rosario would welcome all the help we can give him."

"Good," I said, and went out to ask Marti to call in the full team.

Special Agent Warren Rosario was immediately able to put to bed one of my concerns. I had commandeered the commissioner's meeting room in the courthouse across the street, and ten of us were gathered around the long walnut conference table. Rosario had agreed to allow Marti to take notes, and both state patrolmen had joined us.

Rosario grinned widely at the assembly, giving no indication of feeling rushed or harried. I decided what seemed like a "once-in-a-career" case to a little county department like mine was probably routine to an agent who spent his life in counterterrorism. But I would have appreciated a little more sense of urgency.

"Looks like the perfect day to try to pull off a major heist somewhere in town," he joked, adding to my irritation. He saw my jaw tighten and immediately sobered. "But we've got some serious work facing us, and I appreciate all the cooperation. First, let me take one thing off your plate. Watching about a month's worth of video, we were able to determine that a worker at the munitions plant in Iowa was smuggling M183 kits out of the plant by putting a few at a time in a trash bin. They have a dumpster outside the fenced compound so the garbage crews don't have to bring their trucks onto the secure property. But employees pass through the gate unchecked when they dump trash. Stupid oversight, but that kind of thing happens. The guy was sneaking the kits out to the dumpster, then picking them up at night before the trucks came by." He paused long enough for questions, but we all sensed he wasn't through with his story.

"These kits were marketed on the dark web. We were able to convince the employee—a civilian, by the way—to give us his buyer list. One was a survivalist family from up near Stockton, Missouri. It seems Mid-Missouri Water had a project there pretty much like this one. Property obtained through eminent domain, a couple of suits in court that went against the plaintiffs, and some really angry people, including this family."

I was beginning to see where this was headed and felt a twinge of disappointment. Rosario confirmed my suspicion.

"These people knew that if they tried to get back at Mid-Missouri up in their own area, they'd immediately be suspect. So they hit them down here. The arrests were made this morning and haven't hit the news yet. But they were your dam-busters. As coincidental as it all was, that body being blown into that tree was just that. Pure coincidence. And a stroke of luck for us."

"So these people had no connection at all to Farid Sayegh?" Joseph asked.

Rosario shook his head. "We don't believe so. No connection to Syria, or the Sayeghs, or this part of the state. Just a beef against Mid-Missouri Water."

Similar disappointment tightened the faces of Grace and Joseph. A connection would mean another avenue to finding Sayegh's killer. The Bureau's find left us only Jason Anzar.

I asked what I knew the rest of the team was wondering. "What have you been able to learn about this Qasim Sayegh?"

Rosario pulled a small notebook from a jacket pocket. "Some of this I learned after I got to Springfield," he said. "Farid does have a brother named Qasim who hasn't been seen around Idlib for the last three weeks. A Qasim Sayegh entered Canada on a St. Kitts passport a week ago. The information on the Arbor Suites registration gave him a Columbus, Ohio address. There's a Syrian family at that address that claims him as a visiting uncle. Our contact with them also occurred this morning, so there hasn't been any time to verify their story. According to the woman at the address, Uncle Qasim is off seeing parts of America he's always wanted to visit. No specific itinerary. Given the information we have, there are no solid grounds for detaining the man." Rosario tucked the pad back into his pocket and looked the group over expectantly.

"Did he enter the US legally?" Johansson asked.

"We're checking with Immigration now. It's possible he used the St. Kitts passport to enter the US legally. Or had one under another name."

"He'll know you're on to him," I suggested. "Whoever this is in Columbus will have called him."

"Probably. But our agents didn't indicate to the woman that we know where he is."

I sniffed skeptically. "That just means he'll try to act fast. He won't think he has much time. Has anyone been able to find Jason Anzar? Or figure out who these Talismen are?"

The agent's brow knitted. "Now, that's been an interesting investigation in its own right. This group seems to exist in cyberspace, but we haven't been able to work our way into it. We've no idea who or what they are. Very professionally encrypted communication. Beyond what you would expect from a group of amateur vigilantes. And Anzar has disappeared. So has the van he was driving."

Grace entered the conversation. "Without knowing where Anzar is, and without being able to pick up this new Syrian guy right now, what do we do to protect our families?"

As we'd waited for Rosario to arrive, that was the question that had been eating at me. Suppose we stopped Qasim Sayegh. Or what if Anzar got to him first and replaced one killing with another? What would we have accomplished? If the Sayegh family was willing to send two brothers seven thousand miles to avenge a death, what would they do when a second family member didn't return? The history of the Middle East is one of tribal disputes and family warfare. Were we just bringing an unending chain of honor killings into our county? I decided this was the right time to keep that from happening.

"Protecting the families won't be enough," I said firmly. All heads turned in my direction. "If Qasim fails, there will be another try. If he succeeds, I can easily see one of the Haddad brothers feeling the need to defend the honor of the family by going back to Syria and doing the same thing. It will start a never-ending cycle of killing and retribution."

Rosario studied me for a long moment. "You know the region better than anyone here, Sheriff," he said finally. "And I understand your concern. But what options do we have?"

I looked from him, to Joseph, to my own team who stared at me expectantly.

"It needs to end with this attempt," I said. "We need to let him get to Yusef Haddad."

20

The challenge, or I guess I should say one of the challenges, of arranging the death of Yusef Haddad and restoring peace to the valley, was that there were so damn many moving parts to this whole mess. Even with the explosion out of the equation, we had Haddads scattering to work, school, and play every day; a suspected assassin we couldn't find a good reason to arrest; and an assassin of the assassins we couldn't find at all. It was this last piece I found the most unnerving as we broke up our strategy session and handed out assignments.

Grace was to go to the Haddads and ask them to curtail activities of all three families for the time being, saying only that we were concerned that there was the possibility of a new threat. Rosario feared, and I agreed, that if the local Syrians knew someone specific was after them, they would initiate a first strike of their own. Not what we needed if we were trying to de-escalate.

Rocky D'Amico accepted school duty for the Haddad grade school children. He was to meet the kids at their cluster of apartments each morning, walk them the eight blocks to school, and meet them at the end of the class day. Frankie was to follow the bus with the older kids out to the junior high/high school and trail them back in the afternoon.

Joseph arranged to get another patrolman assigned to the county for both day and night duty, while Johansson and Holland traded shifts keeping an eye on the Arbor Suites and our newly arrived Sayegh brother. Rosario insisted on being free to go where he felt he was needed but agreed to chaperone the men to and from work at Kilgore Homes at 7:30 and 5:00. Grace grumbled about having the unsatisfying assignment of running the office, but still faced two more days of limited activity. Joseph and I took on the task of

145

figuring out why we didn't see anyone else watching Qasim Sayegh.

I couldn't place the Arbor Suites among the dozens of hotels that had sprung up in Springfield since I'd haunted the city as a teenager. Joseph explained that it was just north of the James River Expressway in the burgeoning part of town called the Medical Mile. I suggested I follow her back to her apartment in my pickup, she park the Tahoe and change into civvies, and we go take a closer look at Arbor Suites. Though it was likely that a Syrian, new to the country, wouldn't recognize a blocky, white, unmarked Tahoe with a driver's side spotlight for what it was, there was no sense taking the chance.

Our first pass down Independence Street convinced me our Mr. Sayegh hadn't been quite as clueless in his choice of lodgings as Joseph had suggested. The hotel backed on a highway that could be frantic at rush hour, and he was no more than a quick quarter mile from the onramp. Arbor Suites was a favorite of families wishing to be close to patients at the dozens of medical facilities clustered in that part of town, so people moved in and out at all times of day and night. Clerks expected a mix of visitors and knew not to ask too many questions. The outside rooms meant someone wishing to be anonymous never had to pass the desk. But Joseph was right about one thing. A single drive exited the parking area onto Independence. A stakeout had only to know what vehicle to watch for and keep an eye on the drive.

Newish buildings on three sides of the hotel housed professional services: a dental practice, a diagnostic services center, a cardiology clinic, and the offices of a regional senior living management group. Across the street, partially hidden by a low grassy berm, a veterinary hospital peeked between two mature maples and a scattering of younger spruce. I looped into the lot at the Arbor Suites and parked in the first available spot that faced the street.

"One of us better walk in and spend a few minutes," I

suggested. "If someone's watching the drive, we need to look like a couple wanting a room."

Joseph grinned over at me slyly. "This was creative, Tate. Are you going to come back out and tell me it might be a good idea for us to stay over?"

I shrugged. "Maybe there will be a room next to our guy. We can keep an eye on him and let your men get back to their normal duties."

"Yeah. Right," she sniffed. "And we'd have our attention completely focused on what was going on next door. I think we'd better stick with our assignment."

"Worth a try," I chuckled. "Why don't you go in so I'm not tempted to book the honeymoon suite?" Joseph slid from the pickup and crossed the lot with the look of a woman resigned to a hotel stay while a loved one was receiving treatment. I scanned the lots around and quickly picked out Johansson parked beside the Dental Solution clinic to the east in his equally innocuous white Chevy Tahoe with driver's side spot. If Jason Anzar was watching the hotel and had any surveillance experience at all, he'd know he had company.

I had come to believe that when Anzar was tracking the first Sayegh, he hadn't been alone. The Patrol had checked Farid's room and found no bugs or motion sensors that would alert an outsider when someone moved in or out. Hallway cameras showed only Sayegh and the cleaning woman enter. The frightened girl, a Somali immigrant working on a green card, had convinced Joseph that she knew nothing about the room's occupant and hadn't even seen the man.

My theory was that the Mercedes Sprinter had served as a mobile command post, allowing Anzar to position himself as needed to watch the Syrian's car. That meant he had a roommate. The guy couldn't watch around the clock. Someone switched off with him while he ate, slept, and did whatever else kept his eyes off his mark. So if Qasim Sayegh was being tracked as his brother had been and there was no Sprinter, I should be looking for another van—something two people could live and sleep in for a couple of days. From where I sat in the parking lot, I could see three.

A white Dodge Caravan was nosed into a spot along the front of the hotel, showing what looked like an Oklahoma plate. At the dental clinic, four spots down from Johansson's Tahoe, a red Chrysler Pacifica with Missouri plates faced the hotel, separated by a strip of grass and low shrubs. In front of me across Independence Street, the deeply-tinted windshield of a silver minivan peeked over the grassy berm that separated the road from the animal hospital. The knoll covered enough of the van that I couldn't make the plate or model. A low western sun gleamed off the reflective tinting, shielding anyone who might be watching from the front seat. Both the Dodge and Chrysler looked empty.

I casually picked up my cell and auto-dialed Dave Johansson's number. He answered on the first ring.

"Well, good afternoon, Tate. I see you and Officer Joseph have decided to give me a hand."

I rolled down the window and leaned an elbow against the frame. If I was being watched, this needed to look like a relaxed conversation between friends.

"While you're keeping an eye on our visitor, we're trying to ID anyone who might be doing the same thing. How long have you been here?"

"I came straight up from the briefing. Got here about two. The man I replaced said Sayegh was still inside. He hasn't moved since."

"Where's his car?"

"About six spaces to your left. That dark blue Hyundai."

"I can see three vans that might be mobile surveillance posts. That red Chrysler to your left in the same row, a white Dodge behind me along the front of the hotel, and one I can just see the top of across the street in front of me. Did you see any of them come in while you've been here?"

"Yeah. The red van in this lot has only been here about an hour. A mom with a couple of kids who went into the dental clinic. And that Pacifica got here not too long before you did. An older couple. The woman was driving and unloaded a wheelchair from the back for the man. They must be staying over there while he gets some kind of outpatient treatment."

"And that silver van across from me in the vet hospital lot? Was it there when you got here?"

"Yes. It's been there the whole time."

"Did you happen to ask the officer you replaced about any of the other cars around?"

"No. He just confirmed the guy we're watching for was still in the hotel and pointed out the car he's rented."

"Could you get in touch with him and see if he remembers that van being there?"

"Sure. Give me a minute. I'll be right back with you."

Joseph opened the passenger door as I hung up and slid in beside me. "I see Dave's over by the dental building," she said. "The clerk pointed out Sayegh's car to me. He can see it from the lobby. It's that blue Hyundai. It hasn't moved since he got here."

I nodded. "I just talked to Dave. And keep looking at me while I tell you this. I was asking him about the silver van that's parked almost in front of us across the street. Behind that little mound. He's checking with whoever had the morning shift to see how long it's been there. Until he calls back, you need to be telling me all the rooms are booked."

She gave me a sober, discouraged look. "Sorry Tate. You're out of luck. No room at the inn. In fact, Sayegh was lucky to get one as a walk-in last night."

"No room at the inn? Now, that's an unusual Christian allusion for a Jewish girl from St. Louis."

She gave me a frustrated shake of the head. "Tate, sometimes you come up with the damnedest things—and at the strangest times. What has that got to do with anything? I grew up surrounded by Christmas. I probably know that Christmas story as well as you do. Now, what's going on with the van?"

I was halfway through my theory of two watchers and a mobile surveillance van when Dave called back. I put him on speaker.

"Garcia said the van was there when he picked up the shift at eight," he reported. "He suggested you call Officer Nichols who came over as soon as the hotel reported Qasim's arrival. He covered the night hours."

Joseph glanced at her watch. "I'll call Ron. He should be up by now."

We signed off with Johansson. I started the pickup and pulled out of the Arbor Suite's lot while Joseph dialed. We turned left along a long bend in Independence Street, passing two entrances into the veterinary clinic. When out of sight of the van, I swung into a third drive that led to the back of the building. Nichols answered and Joseph asked about the van while I tucked the pickup in next to a walk that ended at what looked like a rear service entrance.

"Very helpful, Ron," Joseph said as I killed the engine. "I'll let you know what develops." She tucked the phone back into a front pocket of her jeans and gave me a thoughtful frown. "Ron saw the van drive into the lot about six a.m. But he's pretty sure it was parked over in front of the FSL building before that."

"FSL?"

Joseph nodded toward the front of the clinic. "Foster Senior Living. It's the main offices for a group of managed senior living facilities. Just west of the hotel."

"So the van moved from one lot to the other right around six?"

"That what he thinks."

I pushed open the door of the truck. "My turn this time. I'm afraid if I go around the building, whoever's in the van might pick me up in a mirror. I'll see if I can get in through the back and find a window where I can see the plate. If the people inside don't want to cooperate, I may need to have you come in and show your patrol credentials."

"We could both go," she suggested.

I tossed her the keys. "We could. But if the van left while we were in there, we'd be kicking ourselves. If it takes off for some reason, follow it."

The rear door of the clinic was locked. I banged with a fist, waited a few seconds, and was about to risk walking around to the main entrance when a young woman in blue scrubs opened it and peered out, looking embarrassed on my behalf.

"I'm sorry, sir. But this isn't a customer entrance."

I showed her my badge and used my polite officer voice. "I'm with the sheriff's department. We're trying to keep an eye on a van that's parked in your front lot facing the road." As I had guessed, she didn't look carefully at the badge to check the county. "Can I just walk through and take a look out a front window? We're trying to get a plate number."

A concerned frown wrinkled her face. "Oh. Okay. One of the doctors asked when he came in this morning if anyone knew who that was. It was parked there before any of us got here." She held the door and let me into a short hallway that led between two examination rooms into a spacious reception and waiting area. An older man in a white lab coat stepped out of one of the rooms, looked us both over, and asked, "Is there anything I can help you with?" I again showed my badge and explained about the van.

"What's it suspected of?" he wanted to know.

"Several businesses along the street have reported it staying in their parking areas overnight," I improvised. "We're concerned about someone living in it. We don't want them hanging around the area after the buildings close. I'd like to run a check on it before we approach to see if we can learn anything about the owner. A quick look at the plate is all I need, if you don't mind."

"Not a problem for us," he said. "Stacy, walk him on through the kennel room, then back when he has what he needs."

I thanked him and trailed Stacy down a longer hall and into a large open room that smelled of dog chow, woodchips, and antiseptic. Cages against one wall held an assortment of dogs: two sleeping, one pacing and barking anxiously, the rest perched eagerly on their haunches with tongues hanging out. A glassed-off section held cats in smaller cages, all sitting near the front of their pens, watching us suspiciously. It confirmed what I'd always thought about one of the differences between the species: dogs are social creatures; cats are forever wary.

"Are we in any danger?" the girl asked as she guided me across the room to a row of high windows that looked out onto Independence Street.

"I wouldn't think so," I assured her. "With it parked down in this area, we suspect it's someone with a patient in one of the hospitals around who just doesn't want to spring for a hotel. If that's the case, we'll help them find a campground where they can park overnight."

The windows were high enough that the girl had to stand on tiptoes to see the van. "That one there? The silver Toyota?"

"That's the one."

"Does that plate say Mississippi?" she asked, craning to see over the sill.

"Looks like it to me." I copied the number from the light blue plate centered by a round state seal. "Can you read that? Hinds County? I think that's Jackson."

"Yup. Hinds. That's a long way to come for treatment," she murmured.

"They must have family that lives in the area," I suggested.

"Yeah," she agreed. "Don't be mean to them."

21

We waited in the pickup while Joseph called in the license number. It only took seven minutes for the reply. Tyler Brawn of Jackson, Mississippi. She immediately called Rosario, told him what we'd found, and asked if he could get a complete profile run on the name, specifically military service and any connection to the online Talismen. He said he'd try to be back with us within thirty minutes, to hold tight. We filled the half hour by planning how we should approach the darkly tinted van.

It took forty minutes for Rosario to get the information. "Just what you'd suspected," he said, speaking through the Bluetooth in his car. "I'm on my way up there. Tyler Brawn was with the 155th Armored Brigade and served in Syria at the same time Anzar did. He was discharged about three months ago. And his online search history shows connection with the Talismen website."

Joseph chuckled. "How did you find that out so quickly?"

"When you have any kind of presence online, like Facebook," Rosario explained, "it's not that difficult to trace an activity back to a computer's IP address. I'm not sure exactly how our tech team does it, but they can then pretty easily find out what sites that address has accessed. Those search engines aren't any better protected than most good commercial sites, and our guys are good."

Joseph looked over at me with an impressed arch of her forehead. "Do you want us to wait for you to get here to approach the vehicle?" she asked the agent.

"No. I'm still an hour away. Both of you approach. Ask Johansson to keep an eye on you. I'll be there as quick as I can."

Joseph called Dave Johansson while I drove back out of the rear lot and into the clinic's front parking area. "Better reposition where you can see both the hotel drive and this van," she instructed her patrol colleague. "And where you can block this drive pretty quickly if we run into trouble." Dave was moving before I eased my Ford up behind the Sienna.

Joseph released her holster strap as we stepped from the pickup. I approached the driver's door, she the passenger side. The windows were so deeply shaded we couldn't see a damn thing inside the van. I rapped sharply on the driver's window. It immediately whirred downward.

A young man I placed in his early twenties with a square, clean-shaven jaw, intelligent hazel eyes, and close-cut brown hair, grinned out at me. "Something I can help you with?" he asked.

I showed him my badge. "We've had complaints that you've been loitering around the parking areas here. You're making some of the businesspeople nervous." He glanced over his shoulder in the direction of the clinic, then took my badge and looked it over thoughtfully.

"Aren't we in Greene County, Sheriff?" he asked pleasantly. "You seem to be out of your jurisdiction."

I nodded toward the other side of the van. "My partner there is state police. She'll be happy to show you her creds."

"Wow! State police!" he said with a twisted grin. "That's pretty heavy backup for loitering. Especially when I'm not even in your county."

I ignored the sarcasm. "May I see your license, Mr. Brawn," I asked. A voice answered from the rear of the van.

"I'm Brawn. And sure. You can see my license."

I took a step back from the door. "Why don't you both climb out so we can talk a little more comfortably? And anyone else who's in there." The man in the driver's seat eased open the door and stepped onto the pavement. He was four or five inches shorter than I am, 5' 10" or 11", with a gym-junkie kind of build and a T-shirt designed to show it off. The sliding door opened on the passenger side and Tyler Brawn emerged, looked with amusement

154

at Joseph, then gave me a friendly nod across the top of the van. Joseph leaned through the door, glanced around the interior, then gave me an "all clear" bob of the head.

I stepped off the pavement onto the grass of the knoll and nodded for both men to join me. Joseph trailed Brawn but stayed beside the front fender of the Sienna.

Brawn was taller, with the same military cut to his blond hair and a lanky frame. He moved with a slow, sullen saunter that suggested he was a guy who did things when he was damn good and ready. I took an immediate dislike to the man and turned my attention to his partner.

"You must be Jason Anzar," I guessed. Both men's eyes shifted toward me in a moment of surprise, but their expressions didn't change. I watched for them to exchange a quick glance, but it didn't come. Instead, the shorter man studied me for a long moment, bending his mouth into a thoughtful frown.

"Well, this is obviously more than a loitering concern," he said finally, looking casually around until he fixed on Johansson's Tahoe that had eased into the first of the clinic's drives. "And this may be way more than you want to get involved in. Why don't you tell us what you really want from us?"

"Are you Jason Anzar?" I pressed.

"And if I am?"

"Then I'd like to know what the two of you are doing here, and why you were parked like this in a Mercedes Sprinter about a month ago at the Hampton."

"We've got family in the hospital here. We're trying to stay close without paying for a hotel."

I nodded. "Which hospital? And who's the patient?"

"I don't think there's any reason we need to tell you that, Sheriff. It's really none of your business."

"What I think is that your being here has nothing to do with sick relatives."

"Then you must have some other theory. Why don't you tell us what it is?"

"I suspect it has something to do with two Syrian visitors who have been in town at the same time you've been here. Am I right?"

Anzar's frown relaxed, but the crease between his brows remained. "I don't believe you gave us your name, Sheriff? Or your friend's here?"

"I'm Sheriff Tate. This is Officer Joseph. That's State Patrolman Dave Johansson over in the Tahoe. Farid Sayegh's body was found in my county, so I have a special interest in all this."

The crease became a momentary arch of surprise. We had managed to keep Sayegh's identity and the story of his body being blown from the dam out of the media. Anzar obviously didn't know the body had been found. He gave a dismissive snort.

"We don't have any idea what you're taking about," he said calmly.

I looked over at his partner. "What about you, Brawn? Do you know what I'm talking about?" The lanky man shrugged, looking back quickly to see where Joseph was. "No idea," he said, satisfied that she wasn't closing in on him.

I stepped back toward the Sienna. "Mind if we take a look in your van? If you're just hanging around, that shouldn't be a problem."

Anzar stepped with me, keeping himself between me and the driver's door. "It's no real problem, but no. You can't look in."

"Why do you care, if you're just here for a sick family member?"

Anzar put his hand on the door handle. "Maybe because it's a mess. Maybe because we just don't like the idea of two cops trying to do what they know they don't have any right to do. Your partner there already looked inside, which was more than she had permission to do." He gave a quick head nod toward Tyler Brawn. "I think it's time we were moving on—unless you have some real reason for keeping us."

I pressed in close enough that he couldn't open the door. "Why don't you tell us about the Talismen?" I said.

Anzar stepped back and again pursed his lips, staring at me intently. Then he reached for his pocket. I slipped my hand over the grip on my weapon.

"Relax," he said. "I'm just getting my phone. I think I can take care of this with a call." He pulled out the cell, hit three numbers with his thumb, and held it to his ear. Someone answered immediately.

"We have a situation here, Sir," he said. "Some local sheriff and a state patrolwoman are giving us a hard time. I wouldn't have called, but they aren't giving up on us and asked about the Talismen." He listened, then said, "Yes, Sir," and slipped the phone back into his pocket. Then he leaned silently against the van as if waiting for me to speak. I didn't.

For a full minute, the four of us stood like statues, seeing who would flinch first: Brawn with hands in pockets and head tilted to one side; Joseph with eyes darting from one of the men to the other. I finally gave in.

"Are you going to tell us about the Talismen?"

Anzar jerked his head in the direction of Joseph. "I'm waiting for her to get a call."

It came in less than five minutes. She glanced at the display, then said, "Officer Joseph," officially into the phone. As she listened, her eyes continued to move from one of the van's occupants to the other, her expression grim. "Yes, Sir," she said finally and punched the connection closed.

"Let's go, Tate," she said sharply, tilting her head toward the pickup. "I'll fill you in later."

Anzar's expression remained stoic. No smile. No gloating. Just a silent mask.

"Stay out of my county," I warned as I turned to follow Joseph back across the lot. "And move your van. You're making the people inside nervous."

We stopped in front of the Ford without getting in. "That was the Superintendent," she said soberly. "My top boss. All he said was 'Leave the guys alone and don't ask questions.'"

I shook my head. "Who called him?"

"He didn't say. But it was obviously someone he had to listen to."

"Does he have to listen to anyone other than the governor?"

"You figure it out," she said testily. "All I know is we need to leave the guys alone."

22

By the time Rosario pulled in beside us in the Dental Solutions parking area, he had also received a call. We joined him in Johansson's Tahoe.

"Mine came from the Director," he muttered. "I have no idea what the hell's going on. When those of us in counter-intel don't know about this Talismen group, something's pretty screwed up."

I watched the silver Sienna leave the veterinary hospital lot and disappear down Independence Street, heading west.

"He didn't tell you who they were, or he didn't know?" I asked.

"He didn't say. But from his tone, my guess is that he didn't know. He sounded as pissed as I am."

"Who could give him that kind of order?"

"The Director of National Intelligence. Possibly the Attorney General. Or the President, of course."

Joseph shifted uncomfortably on the seat beside me. "That guy could make one call that moved through channels that fast? Hardly seems possible."

"He obviously has some kind of hotline," Rosario said. "And you can bet your sweet ass they won't stop watching our target."

"I'll assume that comment wasn't directed at me," Joseph said coolly.

Rosario reddened. "You're right. A figure of speech I need to quit using. My apologies."

I jumped in before Joseph could take another swipe at the agent. "But you're right. They won't give up. The question is, how will they keep watching?"

A drone swooped high overhead from the direction of the park north of the veterinary hospital and settled on top of one of the pillars supporting the peaked awning that covered the hotel's entrance. As we watched, a camera strapped to its underbelly swung in our direction.

"Well, Tate," Rosario muttered. "There's your answer. The sonsabitches can watch from anywhere around here. They're looking at us right now."

"So," Joseph pressed. "What do we do about our plan?"

Surprisingly, the special agent looked at me. "I've been given an order. Officer Joseph has a direct order. Unless you get a call from your county officials, you haven't been given an order. I think we need to leave this in your hands, Tate." I liked the way he thought.

"I suggest we move ahead as planned," I suggested. "Is Yusef still taking his morning jog through the park along the creek? That's the obvious place for him to get hit."

Rosario nodded. "He won't give it up. And he won't agree to let me run with him. He says he uses it as his own form of prayer."

"But you *do* follow him?" I confirmed, wanting to be certain nothing had changed from our agreement shaped at the courthouse.

"I follow. But far enough back someone could hit him from fifty yards away and be gone into the trees before I could get to them."

"Then we stay with the plan."

"Who's got these Talismen characters?" Joseph wanted to know, staring up at the drone.

I raised a quick hand. "That needs to be me. I'll find the guys and stay with them. They've got to keep that camera here, watching the drive, and can't be far away if they plan to trail Sayegh when he moves. Joseph, why don't you join the other patrol officers in keeping an eye on the hotel."

She gave me a skeptical frown. "There are two of them. If they split up at some point, you can't follow them both."

"And we can't have you messing this up by having your commander learn you've disobeyed an order. Grace should be ready for active duty. I'll bring her back in to work with me."

Joseph's frown turned cynical. "Is she equal to this?"

I didn't like her tone. "She can hold her own with any of us," I insisted. "Could you have Agent Rosario take you back to get your car? I need to start looking for our Talismen."

Instinct, and a little common sense, told me the Mississippi trackers wouldn't stay with the silver Sienna. That meant one of two possibilities. They had the Sprinter somewhere in the city and would switch to it, or they had to buy, steal, or rent another vehicle or have someone bring one to them. If the Sprinter was in Springfield, they couldn't afford to leave the area of the Arbor Suites to go get it, risking a move by Sayegh while they were away. They would call a taxi or one of the ride services to take one of them to the Mercedes. But instinct again told me that wouldn't be their move.

Somewhere over in the parking area for the Hulston Cancer Center or in Schaible Lake Park just north of the vet clinic, a conversation was going on just like the one I was having in my head. If the Sprinter was in town, Tyler Brawn might suggest a switch. Then Jason Anzar would point out that I knew he'd been in town when Farid was killed and had the Mercedes. Trading one marked vehicle for another didn't gain them anything. In fact, the Sprinter was even more distinctive. They needed to be in something we wouldn't recognize and had to get it without compromising surveillance of the hotel.

I swung the Ford out of the dental office parking lot and turned east, knowing I would be watched by the drone until out of sight. The sun had dropped below the horizon in the west, leaving a thin strip of velvety rose just above the line of trees in my rearview mirror.

"Call Grace Torres," I ordered my Bluetooth, checking my lights to make sure I'd left them on auto.

Grace answered before I heard the first ring.

"You ready for a little action?" I asked, turning north at the light onto Freemont.

"Beyond ready," she muttered. "What do you need?"

"I need you in Springfield as quickly as you can get here. But in your Cherokee. And wearing civvies."

"Where should I meet you?"

"Call as you get close. I may be on the move."

"The Jeep's here at the office, and I have clothes in it from when I was at Joseph's. I'll change and be there as quick as I can."

I took the first left onto East Bradford Parkway to loop across the north side of the park toward the cancer center.

"Speed," I suggested. "There's really no one down there to catch you right now."

"Anything special I need to bring?"

"Don't take time to get anything. We'll probably be spending the night in your car and can get something to eat here."

"On my way," she said.

I guessed the Sienna would be where it could quickly get onto James River Expressway if the drone saw Sayegh leave the hotel. The most likely place was somewhere along the south end of the cancer center. I took the ramp up onto the top level of the north parking garage. The open upper deck held only a dozen cars, and I slipped into a spot against the concrete rail. From the barrier, all of the small lake and walking trail that made up Schaible Lake Park were clearly visible in the evening light. Those using the trail parked in the line of cars directly below me, nosed against the grassy border and sidewalk that separated the cancer center from the parkway. As I studied the layout below, powerful halogens on poles as high as the parking garage flickered on along the walk, lighting the strip and boulevard like midday. I ran my eyes along the line of vehicles, settling on the silver van that filled a spot near where East Bradford met Independence Street. The men had positioned themselves for a quick exit if their drone camera showed Sayegh on the move.

I tried again to slip mentally back into the conversation that must be going on inside its dark interior. Steal a car? Too risky.

The last thing the two men wanted was more attention from law enforcement. Were they calling another of the Talismen to deliver a car? I knew I was playing a lot of hunches, but one told me there was some relationship between the Mississippi 155th Armored Brigade Combat Team and this bunch. Nothing official, but I guessed the members were recruited from the brigade when they left the service. Bringing a car up from Jackson meant a drive of about 500 miles. Even if someone came from below the Tennessee line near Memphis, it would take a good five hours. I doubted Qasim Sayegh was going to wait that long.

It was just possible that with the warnings we'd been given by our superiors, they would stick with the Toyota. But I didn't think so. Jason Anzar had looked at me like he recognized a guy who wasn't about to get out of the way. They needed to disappear again. That left buying a used car or renting.

I knew Enterprise had two or three neighborhood rental locations in the Medical Mile. If I were down there in that van, I'd have an Uber pull up beside to take me to the closest rental, pay for three days with cash, and ask that they not run my reserve credit card unless the car wasn't returned on time. The thought had no more than gelled in my supercharged brain when a red Honda CRV pulled up behind the van. Jason Anzar slipped quickly from the Toyota and into the SUV. I watched the Honda exit onto Bradford Parkway and followed it out of sight as it drove north around the park.

Grace called to say she was passing the turnoff to Nixa.

"I'm at the Hulston Cancer Center watching our Talismen from the top of the north parking garage," I told her. "I think one just went after a rental car. See if you can find a spot near the main entrance and go into the foyer. From the door, you should be able to see their silver Sienna van. It's pretty close to the exit onto East Bradford. My guess is that not too long after you get here, one of the men will leave the van and walk to some other car in the lot. Follow him and see where the new car is. I'll start down to you as soon as I see the guy move."

Ten minutes later, Grace's black Cherokee turned into the lot below, stopped long enough to let a car back from a spot near the center's entrance, and pulled into the vacated space. She climbed quickly from the Jeep and walked deliberately into the building. My phone buzzed immediately.

"In place," she said, "and I can see the van."

"I saw you drive in. I won't come down until we see what our men are going to do. I don't want to bump into one accidently."

Three minutes later, the drone hovered slowly down onto the grassy border in front of the van. Tyler climbed out, gathered up the drone, and packed it into the back of the Sienna. He glanced casually around, then walked swiftly to the west across the front of the building and out of sight. Grace waited until he'd passed the entrance, then strolled casually back to her car. When she reached it, she stood beside the door, gazed absently down the lot, and pulled out her phone. She turned as it rang and leaned against the car as if reporting back to a family member about what she had learned inside.

"He got into a white sedan. Looked like a Ford Fusion."

"Is it parked where they can see the drive coming out of the Arbor Suites?"

She looked around for a moment until she located the hotel, then glanced back at the white car. "Yes. I'd say so."

"They'll need to come out of that drive behind you," I instructed. "Leave your spot and bring the Jeep down the east side of the center until out of their line of sight. There are a couple of spots below me here where we'll be able to see the exit. I'll be down to join you in a few minutes."

I waited until she found a new vantage point, then wound down through the concrete stairwell, leaving the pickup to fend for itself with the three cars that remained on the roof level of the garage.

23

Five hours is a long time to be closed in the front seats of a Jeep Cherokee with a woman about whom your fantasies have only been limited by a boyfriend who was a mean sonofabitch until you shot him. That, and the fact that you're her boss. I'd like to say the whole situation made me a little uncomfortable. But I'd be lying. From the minute I climbed into the passenger seat, I knew I was going to enjoy the evening.

Grace had slipped off her seatbelt and curled into the bucket on the driver's side like a kitten on a windowsill. She wore soft, black jeans and somehow managed to tuck both of those long legs up under her in a yoga pose that would have crippled me for a week. I left my own belt off and turned with one knee jammed against the center console, my back against the door.

"Could be a long night," I said awkwardly.

"Got anything else to do?" she said, grinning over at me in the muted light of the streetlamps.

"I was hoping to get a little sleep tonight."

"We can trade off. If you want to catch a few Z's, I'll keep an eye on the exit."

"I'm not feeling it now, but we may be here all night. Let me know if you need a rest."

"I'm fine for now," she said. "Tell me what happened up here during the day."

I filled her in on the van discovery, confronting the two Talismen, and the calls from some mysterious power that took Joseph and Rosario out of the equation. "Nobody told them to stop watching the Syrian," I told her, "but to leave the two guys from Mississippi alone. Since no one warned us off, they're our responsibility."

"So, somebody pretty high up knows about these hits and is protecting the guys who are doing it. How can they justify that?"

I'd been wondering the same thing and had come to my own conclusion. "I think some people see the war as existing wherever the enemy takes it. If we're protecting people here who have been on our side and someone comes after them, we do what needs to be done to protect them."

"Why not just arrest the assassins and lock them away?"

"And add to the Guantanamo problem we already have? Plus, I think it would make the public pretty nervous if they knew foreign killers are roaming across America. It's simpler to just have them disappear."

Grace tilted her head to the side. "You sound like you approve."

"I can't say I approve or disapprove," I confessed. "I understand the rationale. If we're at war, why should it make a difference if we eliminate the enemy there or here? If they sent someone to assassinate the President, for example, wouldn't we be justified in taking out the killer?"

"They aren't here after the President."

"No. But after someone who was an important ally. If we can't provide our friends protection, even when they are here, they'll lose faith in us."

"Then why are you concerned about them being here?"

I grinned over at her. "I just don't like this whole mess coming into our county."

We sat for a few moments, awkwardly studying each other's faces. She really was an incredibly beautiful woman. A Botticelli face, hidden away in the rural Ozarks. What was she thinking? *How did this inexperienced guy with no background in law enforcement get to be my boss*? When she finally spoke, her question startled me.

"Why did you come back to Crayton?"

Was she basically asking the same thing? Why did I take a job that should have come to her? I watched her face for some sign of resentment but saw none.

"What do you mean, why did I come back? This is where I grew up. It's always been home to me."

Her quick nod showed that she'd been misunderstood. "No—I mean, I know you grew up in a pretty rough part of the county and didn't have much. Water from a pump. An outhouse out back. Most of those old cabins aren't even there anymore. But you got away. You've been all kinds of places. Like California and New York. And to all those foreign places."

She paused and gave me an amused grin. "And you've learned about all kinds of useless stuff—like that mumbo-jumbo you were talking to Reverend Frazee about. I've never even heard of Gnostics or whatever those people were. I went to college up in Joplin. That's it." Her face again became sober. "That trip I took with you last year when we went to Tulsa after Verl Greaves? That was about as far as I've been from home. Ever. Oh—and to Kansas City a few times because my dad's crazy about the Chiefs. And we didn't even go into the city. Just to the stadium. But I've never been to St. Louis. Never been on an airplane. And you've been everywhere and seen all kinds of things and learned about all those different ideas. But you came back."

There was a longing in her voice that made me want to reach across the console and pull her to me. Assure her that she amazed me with what an intuitive, perceptive woman she was and that she wasn't somehow diminished by being "just Grace from Crayton."

"There's no place I'd rather live," I said instead. "And you can learn all that worthless stuff I throw around with Matt Frazee from books." I paused, then corrected myself. "Maybe I shouldn't say worthless. Knowing about those ideas just makes me appreciate what I have all the more. The people who live here are the best I've ever known. True friends who'd do anything for you. You're lucky to have been able to spend your life here."

"It's hard to know, when that's *all* you've ever seen or known," she said quietly.

I wondered if she knew how amazing she looked and if that was why New York and California had slipped out when she mentioned places she'd never been? I couldn't suppress my own twinge of sadness and remembered Joseph's comment about exposure and appreciation. This was a woman who would appreciate all kinds of things if she knew about them.

"What would you be if you could be anything?" I asked.

She shrugged with a thoughtful frown. "I don't know that I'd want to be anything different. I feel lucky to be chief deputy. Some people don't even think I ought to be that. But I've read about these places and can't help but wonder what it's like to be there." She relaxed forward a bit and smiled, her hands fidgeting in her lap like a five-year old anticipating a surprise birthday gift. "What's been your favorite?"

"My favorite?"

"Favorite place you've been."

The answer was easy. This was one of my "think about it when you're trying to relax and go to sleep" themes. But I'd realized from these night musings that the places had been favorites partly because I was sharing them with Adeena. I spared Grace that detail.

"San Francisco in the U.S." I said. "I was stationed near there when I was with the Defense Language School. It's just got a feel about it I love. Lots of diversity. Easy to walk from one little neighborhood to another—or take the trolley. And there's a view of the Bay or the ocean from almost anywhere."

"Oh, the ocean," she murmured. "I'd *love* to see the ocean. You said San Francisco was your favorite American place. Where else have you really liked?"

The memory pulled my gaze from her intense dark eyes to a couple walking hand-in-hand along the lighted park trail across the boulevard. Adeena and I had strolled like that—across an arched stone bridge and along a cobbled lane that led through Castle Combe in England's Cotswolds. Among the quaint, slate-tiled cottages we'd found a bakery, no more than two small wrought iron tables on a tiny patio in front of a glass display case of fresh-baked pastries, puddings, and tea cakes. We had shared a caramel, date, and walnut pudding and sipped English tea, soaking in the aroma of warm currant buns, still browning in the oven behind the display.

Grace jarred me back into the dark Cherokee. "You must have been with Adeena," she said with an apologetic smile. "I can see it in your face. I shouldn't have asked."

I shook away the apology. "Oh, no. It was a good memory. And you would love this place. It's a group of villages out in the English countryside that looks just like you imagine them to be. Like calendar pictures. We had the perfect day there . . ."

"Mmm," she murmured. "She was so lucky."

I glanced away again, thinking "lucky" didn't include being hitched to a guy who couldn't keep her alive while we worked together. Time to talk about something else.

"Are you hungry? There's a cafeteria in the center that will be open. A stakeout's not a stakeout without coffee and donuts."

Grace straightened and twisted back behind the wheel. "What if the men start to move?"

I nodded toward the Arbor Suites. "The Patrol has someone over there watching. They'll see Sayegh leave as soon as the guys here do. You'd probably better go inside. I can't risk running into them and you might want to get to a restroom while you can. Keep your phone in your hand. I'll call if there's any change. Do you need money?"

She gave me a dismissive glare. "You don't pay well, but I can handle this. And don't you ever need to use the restroom?"

"I was able to go before you got here." I declined to tell her that, in true country fashion, I'd sneaked a leek against the concrete barrier on the top level of the parking garage.

She slipped from the car.

Ten minutes later, she was back with a cardboard tray with two cups of coffee, chicken salad sandwiches on croissants, and a pair of oatmeal cookies the size of saucers.

"Well, this should tide us over," I laughed. "No donuts?"

"They had cinnamon buns, but someone has to be looking after your health," she said lightly. "Oatmeal raisin seems healthy, even if it's not. Now, what do you want to talk about?"

"How about you?" I suggested, ready to move away from memories of bucolic afternoons with Adeena. "Tell me about your father coming up from Mexico."

24

Just after midnight, Qasim Sayegh began to move. Ron Holland was the stakeout at the Arbor Suites and saw him leave the hotel before the Talismen crew noticed him crossing to his car. After two hours of talking about everything we could think of without approaching personal feelings about each other, Grace had taken over the watch while I dozed with the seat fully reclined. Holland's call jolted me upright.

"We have movement," Holland said quietly, as if the target might somehow hear him in the adjoining lot. "Be alert. I'll call Officer Joseph."

Within seconds, the white Ford Fusion edged into sight at the south end of the cancer center lot, hovering near the exit onto Bradford. Grace started the Cherokee, keeping its lights out.

At the intersection, Sayegh's dark Hyundai hesitated, then swung cautiously through the turn toward the James River Expressway. The Fusion slipped out and followed. Grace backed from her spot and eased the Jeep to the exit, allowing two cars to pass before turning after the Ford. Qasim took the first on-ramp and headed west on the expressway in medium traffic.

"If he's headed toward Crayton, he'll take 60 to Aurora, then 39 south," Grace murmured. "That could be good or bad. It'll be harder for him to know if he's being followed if he stays off the country roads. But it will also be harder for the Talismen guys to force him off the road without being seen. Maybe we should get Bobby moving up 39 to intercept. We can switch off with him to change the scenery."

"I'll alert him," I agreed, "but I don't want either of those cars out of our sight until we're sure where they're going. I'll tell Bobby to come in his own car. He can slip in between us a couple of times, but we need to stay right with them."

Grace took her eyes off the Fusion just long enough to give me a sidelong glance. "Do you think they'll try to stop him before he gets to town?"

I shrugged. "I've been trying to get into their heads all afternoon and so far, they've done pretty much what I expected. I'm thinking they won't want to shoot the guy in his rental. Too messy and too hard to hide. They'll try to get to him somewhere where they can dispose of him easily. They probably already have a plan—like they did with his brother."

"Doesn't seem like they would want him to make it all the way to Crayton, then," Graced mused. "He'll be on county roads for the last fifteen or twenty miles. Maybe they'll cut him off then and drag him out of the car."

I disagreed. "The Syrian's gotta have a gun with him. If they force him off the road and aren't willing to shoot the car up, they'll become targets. And he's a pretty experienced warrior. If Sayegh's headed to stake out the Haddads, he'll find a place to watch the apartments and wait. I think that's when our Talismen will try to get him."

Qasim exited the expressway on Highway 60, turning west. He was headed toward Crayton. I called Rosario and told him it looked like everything was in motion. He said he would check with the Haddad families and try to get everyone rounded up at home, then park where he could see the apartments and sit tight.

As we approached Aurora, Joseph called to say she was about ten minutes behind us. "Don said you went west on the expressway, so I guessed our guy's taking 39," she said. "When you get down toward Crayton, tell me where you want me." Before I could answer, Grace interrupted.

"We're at one of the passing lanes and the Mississippi guys are slowing down," she said urgently. "I think they're trying to see if they have a tail."

I quickly "Roger'ed" Joseph, unfastened my seatbelt, and

dropped sideways onto my knees in front of the seat. "Pass them," I ordered. "Tuck in behind Sayegh. If he's slowed down, pass them both. Then turn at Aurora."

"What if they don't?"

"We can go back and pick them up."

She accelerated in the passing lane, looking straight ahead as she passed the Fusion while I pressed my head against her hip.

"Sayegh's slowed too," she murmured. "I think he's doing the same thing—and the Ford is following me around him."

Two minutes later with me still hunched against the front of the seat, we slowed for the light at the Highway 39 intersection. Grace eased the Cherokee into the turn lane.

"The Talismen guys are going straight," she whispered. "They're right beside me. They don't seem to be expecting the Syrian to turn—but he's coming into the turn lane."

"They'll come back and catch up," I assured her. "Keep the Hyundai in your mirror and let Sayegh follow us. I'll call Bobby and have him drop in behind him at Jenkins. When we get close to town, if Bobby's in place, cut off on the Harrison extension. We can beat him to the apartments."

I clambered back into the seat and returned Joseph's call, asking that she park at the town-end of Beaver Creek Park when she reached town and sit tight. "If you're in your state car, keep it out of sight. I think Sayegh's going to park somewhere nearby, and you don't want to be seen."

As we passed through Jenkins, Bobby Lule's white pickup eased onto the highway behind the Hyundai.

"Bobby's picked him up," I murmured. "Take the cutoff."

The McKenzie Apartments, the semi-permanent residence of the Haddad clan, face a greenway across Beaver Creek Road that had once been covered by most of Crayton's low-end rental housing. When what the National Weather Service called "fifty-year floods" began to happen every three or four years, FEMA paid the city to buy up the properties and tear down the rentals.

The one FEMA condition was that nothing could replace them in the flood plain. The result was Beaver Creek Park, a strip of grass, trees, and jogging paths along both sides of a tributary of Mill Creek.

Along with an old VFW hall that has since become a dance studio, the McKenzie property sits high enough up a gradual slope that it escaped mandatory demolition. Across a side street, another set of apartments escaped the razing: a converted two-level motel, now called The Oaks, with eight units on each floor. This lonely collection sits on the edge of town with nothing beyond but twenty acres of cemetery, scattered patches of woods, and small farmsteads.

The Oaks offers its residents two rows of unlit parking in front, facing the McKenzie Apartments, and one dark row across the back. Grace slipped the Cherokee between a pair of resident pickups in the front lot and killed the lights and engine. Within minutes, the Hyundai cruised slowly past the Haddad apartments. Bobby Lule and his white pickup didn't follow. Qasim Sayegh looped into the dark lot on the street side of the dance studio and doused his own lights. No sign of the Fusion.

"Do you think he shook everybody?" Grace murmured in the darkness.

To our right, blocked from the studio by the Haddad housing units, the shadowy silhouette of a car, lights out, rolled silently down the street between apartment buildings, eased into the other end of The Oaks lot, and braked into an open space. A sliver of moon cast enough light to create shadows, but not enough to determine more than ghostly shapes.

"I'd guess that's our men," I ventured. "No one else would come down here lights-out."

"Can they see Sayegh's car from where they are?"

I guessed at the sightline. "I'd say yes. They must know he pulled in by the studio."

"So—what do we do?"

"We wait," I said, and eased my seat back until the narrow brace between windows disguised my own shadow if lights passed on the road in front of us.

The sliver of moon disappeared just after 2:00. Grace dozed in her seat while I kept watch, aided only by a clear, starlit sky and the faint glow of streetlights from the courthouse square a half mile away. A few minutes before 3:00, Sayegh slipped from his car, framed for an instant by a dome light he had forgotten to turn off. I nudged Grace.

"He's on the move," I whispered. She sat up, fully awake, and watched the Syrian cross Beaver Creek Road, then turn right along the jogging path.

"You were right," She murmured. "He knows Yusef walks in the morning and has gone to find a place to wait for him. How did he get that kind of information?"

"Our Talismen knew he was coming into the country, where he was headed, and when he'd get here," I said. "There must be some pretty elaborate intelligence networks on both sides watching these people."

"Where do you think he's going?"

"If he does what I think he will—and so far, he has—he'll cross the creek down where it goes under the road and come back along the path on the other side. He'll want to be where he can see Yusef leave the house, but where he has more cover."

"This early in the morning, that'll put him in a perfect place for the Mississippi guys to get him," Grace said, looking back up the lot. "I wonder if that's where they shot his brother?"

As if on cue, the Talismen eased out of the Fusion and slipped down the row of cars toward the park.

"Here they come," I warned. "Down until they pass." We dropped into the space below the dash, faces pressed side-by-side above the center console. The gear lever pressed hard against one ear and I felt Grace's jaw tense against the other cheek as we heard the men pass behind us. When they were two cars beyond our position, I quietly whispered, "Let's go."

We twisted across the seats and silently lifted the door handles, slipping from the car. I laid my elbows across the top of the Jeep, weapon and flashlight extended. Grace did the same across the cartop beside her. In the dark shadows of the lot, we could dimly see handguns with suppressors dangling from the men's hands.

I snapped on my light. "Stop where you are," I called in a loud whisper, hoping Sayegh was far enough down the path to be out of earshot. "We have weapons trained on both of you." The men halted, circled by a halo of light. They hesitated for a tense moment, then gradually lifted their arms away from their sides.

"Put the weapons on the ground," I ordered. "Very slowly. You have us both nervous enough to shoot if you so much as flinch."

The Talismen slowly turned in unison and squinted into the lights but didn't lower their weapons. "Is that the damn sheriff?" Jason Anzar said. "Are you the dumbest sonofabitch in the world, or do you think you're some kind of hero?" He was also keeping his voice low enough to avoid alerting the Syrian.

"Put the weapons down," I repeated. "I'm no hero, but some people do think I'm a stupid S-O-B. And that should worry you."

"You didn't believe the guy who told you to stay out of our way?" he called across from the middle of the lot in a loud whisper. "You're gonna be in *deep* shit if you try to mess with us tonight."

"Nobody called me, and I warned you to stay out of my county. You're both carrying illegal weapons and I promise you, the local prosecutor and judge here aren't going to care if the Commander-in-Chief sent you if we have a little shootout here."

"I don't think anyone's with you, Sheriff," he said, his voice reflecting a sneer I couldn't see. "Or did you bring that cute little state trooper?"

Grace hissed at him over her car, touching on her own light. "He brought me, and I'm not the cute little trooper. Another stupid

S-O-B, and I've got a bead on your friend there."

"Ah! But another woman cop. Do you think you could shoot one of us, darlin'?"

"*Oh, yes*," Grace snapped, her tone leaving no doubt. "Maybe both of you if Tate doesn't get you first."

One of the men snickered. "Well, Tate. I'll tell you what we're going to do. We're walking back to our car and we're going to have someone give *you* a call that will let you know you just screwed the pooch."

"Wrong," I called. "You're staying where you are and putting down the weapons. On the count of three, if I don't see them on the ground, I'm going to shoot you in the knee, Anzar."

"And I'm going to shoot the knee out of your friend there," a voice said from behind them. It was Bobby Lule. "*One,*" I said, loudly enough for Anzar, but hoping Sayegh was far enough down the creek to be out of earshot. The Talismen exchanged an angry glance, then bent slowly and placed their weapons on the drive.

"Kick them away," I ordered. They both toed the guns a yard in front of them. "Cuff them," I called to Bobby. He emerged from the deep shadows between cars off to the left of our beams.

"I'll need your cuffs, Grace," he said, moving behind Brawn and snapping his set on the man's wrists. "On your knees," he ordered as Grace moved from her position.

"What a bunch of pricks," Anzar snarled as she circled wide of him, Glock trained on his chest. She handed Bobby her cuffs.

"My squad car's behind The Oaks," he said, handing her the keys. "Why don't you bring it around so we have a secure rear seat."

Anzar glared into my light. "This is a case where my one phone call is going to change your life." He spit the words at me across the black pavement.

"Don't bet on it," I assured him. "And you'll get your call. I just can't promise you when."

25

Since the old bank building was constructed before there was any concern about employees having natural light, the rooms we use as cells weren't given windows that would breach the heavily reinforced block walls. Perfect for a jail, but bare and cold as a storm shelter.

It had been a slow week across the county for misbehavior. The judge let Ernie Bonebrake off with a fine and a stiff admonition. We'd had no drug arrests and no family squabbles that needed a night's separation. So we were able to tuck each of the Talismen into his own private suite, complete with stainless steel toilet and narrow cot. We did have better mattresses than the standard, run-of-the-mill jail, but only because they'd been donated when our one furniture store went out of business seven years ago.

I pulled a chair up outside Anzar's bars and glanced at the wall clock at the end of the hall. It was approaching 4:00 a.m.

"I want my call," he snapped from his perch on the bunk.

"In the morning—when the phone exchange opens up," I said lightly.

He looked at me suspiciously. "You're shitting me. Give me my cell phone."

"I've got to keep it as evidence. We need to know who you gentlemen have been calling."

"Why don't you call that top number and find out?"

"Maybe later."

We stared at each other until he began to fidget. "So what are you sitting there for?" he growled through the bars.

"I need you to tell me some things that might make the rest of our night easier."

"I'm not telling you nothing 'til I get my call."

"You're not getting a call until we talk."

"The hell I'm not. I know my rights."

"I'm sure you do. Officer Lule read them to you. But I think we can work something out if you'll give me a little help."

He glared at me without speaking. I took that as a willingness to listen.

"We've been checking on you guys since your first visit to our county and we found the *nazar* with Farid Sayegh's body," I began.

"What the hell's a *nazar*?" he snapped.

"The amulet. The evil eye. The talisman."

The fleeting narrowing of his eyes told me he was surprised we'd pieced so much together. It passed quickly and I had to be impressed with the guy's composure.

"Like the one we found in your pocket when we checked you in here tonight." I held up the amulet and turned it slowly in my fingers. He watched without expression.

"Not the kind of thing most people carry around with them. And I know from our friends at the Bureau that there have been three or four other killings where the bodies had a *nazar* on them. All foreigners. All people who crept into the country to settle some kind of feud with someone our country is protecting." I leaned far enough to look into the next cell. Tyler Brawn sat grimly on his own mattress, listening intently to my story. "Are you with me, so far?" I asked. Neither so much as blinked.

"So here's what I've worked out in my own head about what's going on," I continued. "We know both you men were with the 155th in Syria and now are connected to a group that calls itself the Talismen." I held the *nazar* over in front of Brawn and waved it to get his attention. "I'm guessing that name has something to do with these. You see, I spent my own tour of duty in Iraq and Afghanistan with the Corps. I know what these are." This time, when I leaned over to look at Brawn, I could see wheels turning behind that stoic mask. "I also know that when you're working with friendlies there, you can get pretty attached to those who are putting their lives on the line with you every day—and pretty pissed off if people around them are selling them out."

Anzar had been slouched back against the wall, but now leaned forward. His expression didn't change, but I read the movement as an indication he was paying closer attention. It was time to try to learn who their calls might be going to.

"Here's the problem I'm having," I confided. "You see, I was a Marine interpreter, working every day with the best intelligence that was coming into our squad. I know enough about how intel works in the war zones to be pretty certain no one in your battalion knew when people like the Sayeghs—the family that was informing on the friendlies you were working with—were headed out of the country. They also wouldn't know when they entered Canada using a visa from some Caribbean island, or who their probable target was here. That information had to be coming from someone, or maybe I should say from *some place*, with pretty sophisticated intelligence gathering capability and lots of connections."

I leaned again around to look at Brawn whose mouth had screwed into a tight frown. "Funny thing is," I added, "we have an agent from the Bureau's counterterrorism unit here working with us, and even *he* doesn't know how this is being done."

I rocked my chair onto its back legs and folded my arms loosely. "That agent doesn't know we've picked you up. He's out there keeping an eye on our local man, who Sayegh came here to kill. But I'll bet he could start asking questions that would raise one hell of a stink if he knew we caught you two walking toward the park with silenced weapons." With enough pause for them to think about the possibility, I added, "That's why I was suggesting we might be able to work something out with a little help from the two of you before I have to bring him in on this."

I stood and stretched. "My partners in the office are waiting to call him if I give them the nod. I'm going in to talk to them for a few minutes. Why don't you two talk it over and see if you feel like you want to work out a deal here on the local level or turn this into a national issue. When I come back, we'll see if we need to call Special Agent Rosario in to join the conversation."

From the fishbowl I could see Jason Anzar pressed against the bars of his cell, whispering to Brawn. Grace was propped in her corner where she couldn't be seen from the jail hallway. Bobby sat on the folding chair with a view of the front of the cells.

"Make any progress?" Grace asked.

I dropped into my desk chair and propped my boots up on the cluttered top. "Hard to say. It depends on how badly they want to keep their little operation out of the public eye."

"And whether they believe you'll help them do that," she added.

"Yeah. That too."

"Will you?" Lule asked.

"That depends on what kind of cooperation we can get from them."

He grunted. "Rosario's going to be pretty pissed if he knows we had them, then let them loose."

"He as much as told me to keep an eye on these guys and leave him out of it."

I rose again as Anzar gave me a head jerk to indicate they were ready to talk. I returned to the chair in front of his cell, swung it around, and straddled it, propping my arms across the bowed back. I tried to look in at him with as little expectation as they had shown. The first move needed to be theirs.

"You were a Marine?" Anzar asked.

"Yup. Fifteenth Expeditionary Unit. Ground Control Element."

"And did time in Iraq and Afghanistan?"

"Mainly Iraq. Some in Afghanistan providing interpreting assistance for the Army's Third Infantry."

"So I'd guess you got kind of close to some of the friendlies."

"Pretty close. Yup."

"And didn't see anything wrong with hitting those who were selling out or trying to kill your friends."

"That's why we were there," I agreed.

Anzar pursed his lips and stared at me through the bars for a moment, then asked, "And what if the same thing was happening here? Some of the bad guys were after friendlies we'd brought into this country?"

I shrugged over the back of the chair. "That's what I do. I try to protect my friends from people who want to do them harm."

Anzar gave a quick upward jerk of his head. "But it's not okay with you when we're trying to do the same thing."

"It's not okay when you're in my area, and I don't know what the hell you're up to."

"You pretty well outlined it as it is," he confessed. "We're here after the bad guy. We don't like him coming after people who were trying to keep us alive when we were working with them. Simple as that."

"Not as simple," I objected. "First of all, no one checked with me. And second, when you kill someone in this country, unless it's self-defense, it's murder, even if the guy's a no-good sonofabitch. And hunting him down isn't exactly self-defense. Someone shoots a drug dealer in my county, I have to treat it like every other killing. I leave it to the courts to work out all the 'who deserved what' kind of stuff."

"Even if you know the guy's a snitch and a killer?"

"That's not my job to decide."

Anzar sniffed. "It was when you were a Marine."

"I'm not a Marine now, and this isn't Anbar Province or Idlib. And I don't know who you're working for. I can't have people running around the county taking care of all the little injustices they think exist out there in the world."

"I think you know by now that we're supported by people pretty high up."

"That doesn't mean squat to me. If your plan is to shoot

someone—like you did this guy's brother—you could be sent here by God himself and if you don't check in here with me, you're just a couple of vigilantes."

Anzar slouched back again on the cot, arms folded tightly. "Okay. So we're here checking in. And you've got a man out there who's going to kill one of your precious citizens. What are you going to do about it?"

I straightened on the chair. "I'll tell you what *you're* going to do about it. Nothing for now." I glanced again at the wall clock. "We're going to be leaving you here for three or four hours. When we get back, if all goes as planned, Sayegh will still be alive and will be headed out of town. You tell me a couple of things—just to help me get this all figured out—and I'll let you go then. He'll be all yours. Once he gets out of the county where he isn't my problem, you can do whatever you want with him. We won't say a word. As far as we'll be concerned, you were never here."

"We won't tell you who we're working with. Non-negotiable."

"I don't really care about that, though I am curious. Mainly I want to know two things. How did you get Farid Sayegh buried in the dam, and what were you going to do with Qasim?"

"We tell you that and we're out of here? No other questions?"

"You're out of here in three or four hours."

"Your man will be dead by then."

"That'll be my problem. But when you find Sayegh, I want it to be well outside of this county. We've had enough assassins from Idlib coming our way."

"We can stop him before he gets your man . . . ."

"And what will that do? Just bring another of them over here who might slip through your little net. This all needs to end tonight."

"Tell him," Brawn called through the cell wall. "Let him worry about his guy here. We can still get the man they sent us after."

Anzar stared at me intently for a long moment. "How do we know you're going to do what you say?"

I raised my hands off the chair back. "I saw what you guys can do with a phone call. Why would I want that kind of trouble? I'd just as soon you disappeared and left us alone here."

He nodded grimly. "Okay. It wasn't hard to get the guy into the dam. We had someone check out the area for new excavation sites, and that one looked perfect. We just carried him around the end of that fence, dug out a trench with shovels, and covered him up. The construction crews added another layer the next morning. Who'd have guessed someone would blow the thing up?"

"Yeah, who'd of guessed?" I chuckled. "And no one heard you digging down there?"

It was their turn to chuckle. "We could have used a dozer and that guy wouldn't have heard us. He had some movie playing so loud we could hear it just like we were in that little shack with him."

"And Qasim? What were you going to do with him?"

Anzar smirked through the bars. "You got another project where the county road district is widening one of the roads west of here. Moving a lot of fill. We'd be doing the same thing right about now."

I pushed back off the chair. "Well, we've got some work to do. You two sit tight, and we'll be back when it's taken care of. I've got Lule staying to keep an eye on you. Don't give him a bad time or the deal's off."

"If you don't want a bad time, get us out of here like you said," Anzar growled.

I nodded to Grace who rose and headed toward the outer door.

"You boys behave and you'll be able to grab some breakfast at LeeAnn's on the way out of town," I called over my shoulder.

26

We left Bobby Lule with explicit instructions that the two men were not to be allowed to make a call, couldn't leave their cells for any reason, and shouldn't be given anything to eat or drink unless they were seated back on their bunks.

"I know you can handle yourself, but don't trust either of them," I told him. "Don't give them any opportunity to grab you through the bars. We should be back before eight."

Grace and I looped around Beaver Creek Park and up onto the bluff above the walking trail, leaving her Jeep at the trailhead where dirt bike paths wind through the woods above the creek. The disadvantage an outsider has when being tracked by locals in rural America is that every kid in town, for generations past, has been executing mock attacks and ambushes through every stretch of woods in the county. There had been a time, not too many years earlier, when I could have led a raiding team down that bluff blindfolded without making a sound. The game trails had changed over the past fifteen years, but not enough that either of us had trouble slipping down through the dark shadows of a moonless night in silence.

If Yusef Haddad followed his standard morning routine, he would leave his apartment and head in toward town for just over a mile on the path on the street side of the creek. He'd cross the stream at the Hardy's Mill Bridge, then jog along the wooded side to where the stream passes under Beaver Creek Road. Then back to his apartment to shower and change for work. There were any number of trees on the return side that could hide a man. But my guess was that Yusef's assassin would walk the middle stretch of the path where it was farthest from any buildings, see the giant sycamore that was only five or six paces off the trail and branched into two barrel-thick arms at about shoulder-height, and find it a perfect vantage point.

I sent Grace in a direction closer to the Mill bridge, then took a trail I knew would bring me down close behind the sycamore. My steps were at first slow and measured, knowing that the Syrian was conditioned to waiting in the night silence, probing the air about him for any sound that signaled danger. With each pause, I trapped my breath and listened for Grace, but heard nothing. She and her siblings had also cut their eyeeteeth chasing each other through these woods, sometimes intent on being so quiet that even the crows and jays weren't disturbed.

Then in the distance, I heard the wail of the Kansas City Southern intermodal train, hauling a hundred stacked semi-trailers south toward the Gulf. The barrier where the tracks crossed Beaver Park Road would soon begin to clang, the train whistle would sound two or three long blasts as it approached the crossing, and I'd have three or four minutes of rhythmic, window-rattling clicking as the train rumbled behind The Oaks. I waited for the first whistle burst, then scrambled downward, pausing between the train's wailing screams and reaching the first patch of grass by the time the night again began to quiet.

I was thirty yards from the sycamore. In the first shades of morning gray, the shadowy figure of the assassin crouched against the base of the tree, just where I had placed him. His head lolled forward onto his chest, arms clasped tightly, unfazed by the clatter of the train. I slipped behind a walnut trunk, checked the time on my silenced phone, and waited.

Joseph should now be in position where she could watch the Hardy's Mill Bridge. Grace was midway between the bridge and the sycamore. Rosario would leave his stakeout post near the apartments shortly before dawn and cover the Beaver Park Road bridge behind me. His assignment, with Joseph, was to keep any other joggers or bikers off the trail after 6:00 a.m. With the four of us in place, Yusef should be in sight of someone during his entire jog. My eyes were to stay on Qasim Sayegh.

At 5:55 sharp, a low buzz from a watch on Qasim's wrist stirred the Syrian from his doze. The sky had clouded over as dawn approached and in the muted half-light of an overcast sky, he double-checked the time, then stared for a moment across the creek at the sleeping apartments. After a quick check of the path, he punched a number into his cell and whispered for less than a minute, then slipped around the thick trunk until hidden from the road.

Within two minutes of 6:30, Yusef Haddad stepped through the door of his ground-floor apartment and stretched lazily. He wore a pair of gray unmarked sweats with a kangaroo pouch across the front of the jersey, the hood pulled back onto his shoulders. His dark hair was hidden under a black stocking cap. He looked up at the flat, moody sky, frowned his disapproval, and walked nonchalantly across the street to the paved trail.

Fifty yards across the creek, Qasim flattened against the sycamore, clutching his silenced weapon against his chest. Yusef leaned into a half-hearted quad stretch, first left, then right, glanced at the time on his own watch, and started a shuffling jog toward the Hardy's Mill Bridge.

Qasim edged around the tree away from his target, turned into the Y in the trunk, and practiced steadying his firearm in the narrow crotch. I moved with him, keeping the walnut between us as I drew the Sig and listened to Yusef's retreating steps. The creek was wide and slow here, flowing with just a whisper of moving water. As the morning again became silent, I could hear and feel the muted thumping of my own heart, a sensation I hadn't experienced since trailing my squad leader through a village sweep in Iraq. The night at Marti's when Sal had gone after Grace had been one of constant movement and action. No time to be aware of the fear and throbbing pulse that were part of tense, uncertain waiting.

For nearly twenty minutes, everything along the trail seemed frozen in time: me braced against the back of the walnut fingering my Sig; Qasim peering through the crotch of the sycamore; Grace in her own hiding place, perhaps able to see the two of us; Joseph and Rosario sitting restlessly in their cars guarding access to the path.

In the distance, I heard the rhythmic *pat-pat* of Yusef's shoes as he shuffled toward us on our side of the stream. Qasim heard him at the same moment and rose upright, pressing into the white side of the sycamore where he could swing quickly into position for his shot. I pulled the Sig up against my shoulder and peered around the trunk.

Yusef was a hundred yards away, moving at a relaxed trot, his eyes on the path a few yards ahead of him. His hands were tucked into the long pocket of his sweatshirt. Qasim leaned awkwardly behind one of the trunk's thick branches, weapon tight against his chin.

From further down the path, near where I expected Grace to be hiding, a second runner appeared suddenly from the base of the hillside. He jogged in place for a moment beside the trail, looked quickly in both directions, then fell in behind the Syrian, closing at a brisk pace. He wore a pair of faded orange sweats with the same waist pocket, the hood pulled forward hiding his face. As he reached Yusef, he appeared to mutter a passing greeting, then moved quickly past him in my direction. Qasim now stood with his side toward me, his lips curled into a silent curse.

Twenty paces beyond the Syrian, the second jogger stopped and spun, drawing a silenced pistol from the pocket of his sweats. He squared and fired two quick shots into the chest of the man who was now only forty feet away. In an instant, Yusef's face passed from surprise and terror to pained resignation as he pitched backward, clutching at a crimson stain that spread across his gray jersey.

Qasim again fell into a crouch, glanced about in panicked confusion, then broke into a run in the direction of Rosario and the

Beaver Creek bridge. Twenty yards beyond my hiding place, he turned off the path and sprinted into the trees away from the stream without looking back. Yusef's assailant had also turned toward the hillside and was running in a low crouch toward where Grace must be hiding to intercept. I dashed toward the fallen Syrian, holstering my weapon as I ran. Dropping to one knee beside the bloodstained body, I pressed two fingers tightly up beneath Yusef's jaw.

27

You might say that Deputy Frankie "Rambo" Ritter had been born for this role. For one thing, he looks the part. He's about five-nine, thin, with a hawkish face that just looks sinister. I like to tell people that the first time I visited the man's house up in Willston, I was responding to an anonymous call reporting gunfire in the neighborhood. I'd found Frankie in his back yard, practicing a drop-roll-and-fire maneuver he was trying to perfect using a two-foot high crossbar and a target he'd braced against a pile of sandbags. To my knowledge, he's only used the maneuver once, rolling sideways out of his patrol car into a drainage ditch while backing up a state trooper who had pulled over a suspicious, heavily-tinted black Camaro. Fortunately, the ditch was flooded and a screen of cattails kept him from firing off a shot, or he might be locked up over in Potosi rather than a questionable addition to our force.

So the role of killer had been a natural, aside from a nagging concern on the part of Grace and Marti that he might forget the blanks and accidently kill the man we were trying to protect. It had been Marti's job to meet with Ritter at 6:00 a.m. at the station, make sure Bobby wasn't having trouble with our jailed guests, and check Frankie's load for harmless bullets.

Yusef had initially balked at the plan, believing that if another Sayegh had been sent to get him, he and his brothers should intercept and rid the world of the traitor. But we were able to convince him that the string of back-and-forth revenge killings might never end until one assassin believed he had succeeded and the other side didn't care. Once Yusef bought into the plan, despite his wife Lilia's strenuous objections, he became as committed as

Ritter to play his role to the hilt.

Marti had whipped up two thin pouches of fake blood from a Halloween recipe she'd found online using corn syrup, Hawaiian punch, and chocolate syrup. Luckily, the evidence had stayed intact in the pouch of Yusef's sweatshirt until he grimaced, slapped them hard against his chest, and threw himself backward. The fall had been so authentic he'd momentarily knocked himself out against the paved trail.

Grace joined me almost immediately beside the fallen Syrian, looking like a concerned citizen out for a morning walk. As we crouched over Yusef, she asked again if I was sure I wanted to let Qasim Sayegh escape.

"He needs time to report what's happened," I murmured, looking about nervously as if searching for whoever had gunned down a citizen in a public park. "And we want those he calls to know he made it out of the area before he disappears, should that happen." I pulled out my cell. "I'll call the department. Why don't you get ahold of Chase and get the ambulance over here. We need to move the body just as we normally would. Ask him to run with sirens on."

The coroner and a deputy arrived within five minutes, both driving their vehicles down the jogging path to the fallen body. While Frankie Ritter, now dressed in his service uniform, photographed the scene and kept curious gawkers from The Oaks at bay, Chase checked the corpse for any sign of life, solemnly shook his head, and pulled a gurney from the back of the ambulance. I helped him load the motionless victim.

Joseph and Rosario were waiting at Backman's Funeral Home when Chase arrived, remaining in the reception area until the draped body was wheeled inside. Grace had climbed back up to her Cherokee, scouring the hillside for any sign the assassin had hidden in the trees to watch the scene below. She and Ritter reached the mortuary as the ambulance was pulling up and escorted us inside.

"The woods were clear," she reported. "I suspect our man's still running."

I smiled grimly at the assembled team. "This couldn't have gone better," I said, giving Ritter an appreciative nod. The deputy beamed and extended a hand to the still horizontal Yusef who had pushed the sheet onto the floor, but chose to remain stretched regally on the gurney, rubbing the back of his head.

"Ya almost fooled me there for a minute," Frankie chuckled. "I've never truly shot a man, but if I did, I expect he'd look like you did. We fooled him."

"I can't remember ever being this excited and nervous about responding to a call," Chase said, still a little jittery. "Imagine! An international assassination attempt right here on the edge of town."

I gave him a light slap on the shoulder. "You were great, Chase. Everyone played their parts perfectly."

Special Agent Rosario took my elbow and directed me to the outer door, turning his back to the cluster around Yusef. "You know I can't officially have had anything to do with this," he confided. "I was told to leave that pair from Mississippi alone. I've done that. But I can't very well report that we had a Syrian killer in our sights and let him go. I'm just planning to say that we were able to keep our immigrants safe, and that it looks like we won't have future problems here. I hope you can support me in that."

"As far as I'm concerned," I assured him, "you weren't here at all this morning. The others will agree. And I can vouch for you having left the Mississippi boys alone."

"I'm a little surprised we haven't seen anything of them," he muttered, looking back toward the group who were still celebrating their performance. Yusef was now upright, describing in vivid detail how he had reacted to the shots.

I paused long enough to let Rosario know it wouldn't be wise to say more. "I think I'd head back to Springfield and check in with your home office," I suggested. "You might want to let them know I called, and everything here has been taken care of. Qasim missed his target and disappeared."

He gave me a long, thoughtful look, then nodded. "I was just headed that way. I should be there by nine-thirty."

"That'll be about right. We're all going to have some breakfast over at LeeAnn's before we go back to the office to see if Bobby had to lock anyone up overnight." Rosario shook his head with a bemused grin, gave my hand a firm squeeze, and pushed open the mortuary door, sending a quick wave to the others. The less conversation before he left town, the better.

When I unlocked the cells, Tyler Brawn grabbed the coffee cup from the edge of the wash basin and was out before the barred door was fully open. While we had eaten at LeeAnn's, we ordered breakfast sent over. The coffee was all that was left of Tyler's Sunnyside-Up Special. Jason Anzar stayed planted on the bunk and glowered at me.

"So—what the hell happened this morning? Did you let Sayegh get to his target?"

I scooted the same chair back in front of the open cell and straddled it backward, staring at him sourly. "Yusef Haddad was shot down in the park about 7:00. You probably heard the sirens."

"You let the bastard do it?"

"I wanted this problem out of my county. As long as Haddad was alive, the problem kept coming back."

"You're one cold sonofabitch," Anzar sneered.

"I told you I was an S-O-B. I'm not paid to be warm and fuzzy."

Anzar's eyes narrowed and he glanced through the bars at Brawn, who had come back over to make sure he was hearing all this right.

"So what did the Syrian do?" Anzar asked.

"The dead one or the one you came to get?"

"Our man."

"Turned and ran like hell."

"And you didn't stop him?"

"I told you I wouldn't."

Anzar pushed up from the bunk. "So, where did he go?"

I slid the chair out of the doorway and back against the wall. "No idea. If he checked out of the hotel when he left last night, he could have gone anywhere. If he circled back for his car, he'll still have that rental but could probably turn it in anywhere. He may just abandon it. Like I promised, I left him to you."

I glanced over at the wall clock. "He's got about two hours on you. With all your resources, you should be able to find him before he slips back into Canada. But I figure he's had time to let his people back in Idlib know Yusef Haddad is dead."

Anzar pushed past me and tromped to where Marti had his personal items in a plastic bag. "You might still be hearing from our people," he threatened.

I crossed the office to join him. "That wasn't our deal. . . and I don't think so. We'll be keeping Yusef's obit out of the paper. There won't be anything else to indicate you two were here. It would probably be smartest to leave things the way they are." I pulled the *nazar* out of his plastic bag and tossed it to him. "I think I'd keep this in your pocket. And I wouldn't be coming back into this part of the state again."

Brawn picked up his belongings, Anzar pocketed the amulet, and the pair gave me and Grace a final onceover—more her than me. They left without so much as a "Thanks for putting us up."

"Sweet couple of guys," Grace muttered. "Do you think they'll find Qasim before he can get out of the country?"

I watched them through our single outside window as they cut across the square toward the town end of Beaver Creek Park and their car. "If I had to put money on it, I'd bet on those two and their backup team, whoever that is. They seem to have eyes everywhere. But we'll probably be better off if they don't. I'd like to see the guy get back to Idlib and tell his people in person that Yusef is gone."

"If the Talismen do get to him," Grace wondered, "will that be the end of it? Or will his family send someone over to see what happened to him?"

I put a hand on Grace's shoulder in a way that probably wasn't smart, given today's climate. "I can think of only one sure way to find out," I suggested.

28

The parade that wound its way up Webber's Mountain was the strangest collection to ever visit the sisters. It was led by a tall, Latina beauty who looked like she was modeling a deputy's uniform for some outdoor photo shoot. Behind her, a sturdy woman in full hijab stepped gingerly up the path in what appeared to be light slippers. The pretty, dark-haired girl who followed was nearing twenty. Other than a headscarf, she wore the same ripped jeans and "I'll be there for you" T-shirt that were popular with her classmates in the nursing program she attended. I brought up the rear: boots, jeans without the trendy tears, khaki uniform shirt, and ball cap. The sisters were on their porch, waiting as if a group like ours came for a reading every day and had called ahead.

"Isn't this just the nicest surprise, Edith?" left-handed Ethel said. "And weren't we just saying, 'It's time for that good-looking Tate boy to come pay us another visit.'"

"And I was saying, 'I think that lovely Mexican girl will come with him this time,'" Edith continued without a pause. "And the woman who's had so much family trouble should be coming again soon. And here you all are together!"

They ushered us into the parlor which had already been set for six: four chairs grouped around three sides of their small table, with two side-by-side at one end. A wood fire burned in the enameled iron stove and a kettle was just beginning to whistle.

"Will you all be having tea?" Edith asked, seating Lilia Haddad closest to their chairs on the right and Grace to their left. Raca Haddad and I took the chairs facing them.

"We still have some of that dark tea you brought during your first visit," they said to Lilia. "And you, Grace. It is Grace, isn't it? We have the jasmine tea you liked so much. Can we prepare a cup of the oolong for you, Sheriff?"

I raised a declining hand as I tipped back on my assigned seat, guessing from the way we were positioned that the sisters had anticipated my refusal and were expecting to read for the women.

"Then you and the young lady can choose from what we are fixing for the others," Ethel suggested. "Everyone must have tea. We can all just sit and have a visit for a time. Please, Mr. Tate, tell us how your mother has been." Though they had sensed that we were coming and remembered each of our tea preferences, they seemed to have forgotten since my last visit that mother was long since gone. When I reminded them, they fussed about it as if they were hearing about it for the first time.

While Lilia Haddad looked on with a distant, nervous smile, we chatted about my sheriff's work, Raca's interest in becoming a nurse, and why Grace's father had come to the Ozarks as a teenager from Chiapas to work in the chicken plants. When cups were close to empty, the twins exchanged a glance that signaled it was time for what had brought this unlikely foursome up onto Webber's Mountain.

"Now," Ethel said to Raca. "If you will have your mother pour her last bit of tea onto the saucer and place the cup here between us, the handle toward her, we will see what the leaves have to tell us."

Lilia drained the cup before her daughter had time to speak, setting it carefully between the two seers, the handle in her direction. Edith and Ethel leaned intently forward, peering into the porcelain bowl. After an unnerving moment of humming and murmuring as they studied the scatter of dark flecks, they exchanged another knowing look and Edith spoke.

"We see no danger in the leaves, my dear. Your family will be safe here."

Lilia's eyes welled with tears and she pressed folded hands against her lips, nodding gratefully toward each of the sisters. Raca bent toward her mother and laid a hand on the woman's quivering shoulder, blinking back moisture from her own eyes.

"Do you see anything else for the family?" she asked.

The twins smiled slyly at the girl. "Have you met a friend at school? Someone you care about very much?" Raca looked down with surprised embarrassment while her mother cast her a troubled frown. The girl eased her own cup away from the sisters who tittered like a pair of house wrens. "Perhaps we are mistaken, and you will need to come back for another reading," Ethel said in a failed effort to calm Mrs. Haddad.

"We will talk on the way home," Lilia said in Arabic, then looked quickly over at me, realizing I understood. ". . . or after we get to the house," she corrected. It occurred to me that Miriam Haddad's interrogation when we were driving out to Farley Buzzard's goat farm about loving someone of another faith hadn't been for her benefit at all, but for her sister Raca.

Edith turned to Grace, who now seemed reluctant to offer her cup. "Come, dear," the old woman said. "We know you have also had a very painful time. Perhaps there is comfort for you as well." Grace hesitantly emptied her last drops of tea and positioned the cup between the sisters. The twins fussed over the leaves for a few moments, then Edith reached over and took Grace's hand.

"New love is coming to your life, my dear," Ethel said. "And this will be a kind and loving man." She leaned over and whispered to Edith who nodded with a secretive smile. "And you will have children," Ethel confided. "One will be a beautiful girl like her mother."

Grace is about as stoic a woman as I've known, but the revelation brought a sudden rush of tears. While I was debating whether to reach over and give her other hand a supportive squeeze, Edith lifted my cup and poured the remaining drops onto the saucer. I reached for it, but she shooed my hand away.

"This is a morning of happy news," she said. "Perhaps there is some for you." My thoughts flew to my last reading and the sisters' prediction that my dilemma would resolve itself.

"Let's make it some impersonal happy news," I suggested. Ethel smiled over at me broadly. She and Edith peered into the cup. This time, when they exchanged glances, Edith shook her head and they returned to their examination.

"You have a difficult year ahead of you, young Mr. Tate" Ethel said finally. "Two lost children. A friend who will need your help to save what is most important to him. Travel to a distant place."

I grinned at her nervously. "That doesn't sound like very happy news. Is that all you see in there?"

"All we can see today," she said solemnly." And some things, Mr. Tate, are not for two tired old women to tell."

Visit Allen Kent's website at http://allenkentbooks.com
ALSO BY ALLEN KENT

<u>Unit 1 novels</u>
The Shield of Darius
The Weavers of Meanchey
The Wager
The Marburg Mutation
Straits of the Between
Ring of Thorns

<u>The Whitlock Series (Historical novels)</u>
River of Light and Shadow
Wild Whistling Blackbirds
Suzanna's Song

<u>The Colby Tate Mysteries</u>
Murder One
Eye for an Eye

<u>Other Mystery/Thrillers</u>
Backwater
Guardians of the Second Son

<u>Young Adult Adventure</u>
Switch

ABOUT THE AUTHOR

Allen Kent is the "USA Today" and Amazon bestselling author of the popular Unit 1 thriller series, the Colby Tate Mystery Series, and the celebrated Whitlock Trilogy in historical fiction. His books, with summaries, can be found at his website, https://allenkentbooks.com.